PRAISE FOR JUAN JOSÉ SAER

"A cerebral explorer of the problems of narrative in the wake of Joyce and Woolf, of Borges, of Rulfo and Arlt, Saer is also a stunning poet of place."—*The Nation*

"To say that Juan José Saer is the best Argentinian writer of today is to undervalue his work. It would be better to say that Saer is one of the best writers of today in any language."—Ricardo Piglia

"[*La Grande*] is a daring, idiosyncratic work that examines the idea of an individual person navigating the whirl of random events that helps shape everyone's lives."—*Kirkus Review* (starred)

"The most striking element of Saer's writing is his prose, at once dynamic and poetic. . . . It is brilliant."—*Harvard Review*

"Brilliant. . . . Saer's *The Sixty-Five Years of Washington* captures the wildness of human experience in all its variety."—*New York Times*

"What Saer presents marvelously is the experience of reality, and the characters' attempts to write their own narratives within its excess."—*Bookforum*

ALSO BY JUAN JOSÉ SAER

The Event
The Investigation
La Grande
Nobody Nothing Never
The One Before
Scars
The Sixty-Five Years of Washington
The Witness

JUAN JOSÉ SAER

TRANSLATED FROM THE SPANISH BY HILARY VAUGHN DOBEL

OPEN LETTER
LITERARY TRANSLATIONS FROM THE UNIVERSITY OF ROCHESTER

First edition, 2016
All rights reserved

Library of Congress Cataloging-in-Publication Data:

Names: Saer, Juan José, 1937-2005, author. | Dobel, Hilary Vaughn
Title: The clouds / by Juan José Saer ; translated from the Spanish
    by Hilary Vaughn Dobel.
Other titles: Nubes. English
Description: Rochester, NY : Open Letter, 2016.
Identifiers: LCCN 2015038413| ISBN 9781940953342 (paperback) |
    ISBN 1940953340 (paperback)
Subjects: | BISAC: FICTION / Literary. | HISTORY / Latin America / South
    America. | PSYCHOLOGY / Mental Health. | POLITICAL SCIENCE /
    Colonialism & Post-Colonialism.
Classification: LCC PQ7797.S22435 N813 2016 | DDC 863/.64--dc23
LC record available at https://lccn.loc.gov/2015038413

Printed on acid-free paper in the United States of America.

Text set in Bodoni, a serif typeface first designed by Giambattista
Bodoni (1740–1813) in 1798.

Design by N. J. Furl

Open Letter is the University of Rochester's nonprofit, literary translation press:
Lattimore Hall 411, Box 270082, Rochester, NY 14627

www.openletterbooks.org

"Afford thy desire some time."
—La Celestina, *Act VI*

THE CLOUDS

Prologue

He finds himself already at the corner by the ice cream stand, shielded from the sun by the broad red-and-white-striped awning. Before moving out of the shade to the sunny sidewalk across the street, he anticipates the feeling of heat-softened asphalt beneath the soles of his brown loafers. And now, on the gray sidewalk that shimmers and burns in the summer siesta hour, his shadow pools at his feet as if shriveled by the sun as it finally begins to sink, slowly, from its high point.

He is about to eat a double-scoop of chocolate and vanilla, his unusual lunch, and if he's waited this long to leave his office to buy it—it's nearly two-thirty—it is because he's decided that the ice cream ought to get him by until dinnertime. Doubtless, the heat is the primary cause of such frugality, but a sort of athletic stoicism, as he imagines it (a result of the day's caprice rather than habit), colors this stratagem of his ever so slightly with virtue. So he is pleased for the moment: content, spry, and healthy, and, not yet too far into his fifties, he believes he has great prospects, both immediate and long-term. He feels tall, bright, and vital, as if a red carpet stretched from the tips of his toes on to infinity. But almost immediately the harsh summer weather, the tumult of the street, and the black, noxious exhaust fumes carry him back to reality, to that midpoint in his soul between anxiety and euphoria that acquaintances—and he himself, grown convinced by what began as an idle joke—refer to with unjustified certainty as his temperament.

The heat wave has broiled the city for over a week. From a cloudless blue sky, the sun beats down with a merciless, all-pervading light that scorches the trees, muddies the senses, and dulls the mind. The heat relents only at night, and, then, only a little, but during Daylight Savings Time—*strictly an administrative decision*, he likes to joke, *only until the hens change their minds*—at the year's height, nightfall never ends and dusk lingers until just after 3 A.M.; when everyone's still sleepless on account of the heat, dawn breaks, livid, in the east, and the intolerable sun reappears. Crowds of people lie tanning on the riverbanks, waiting for night, rain, vacation, an unlikely breeze, but the sweaty workers who eye them from the docks or one of the bridges, from the bus or the elevated metro over the Seine, watch the crowds with skepticism rather than jealousy.

It is the sixth of July. Last year, intending to settle affairs with his few remaining friends, Pichón visited his native city for some weeks from mid-February through the beginning of April after a twenty-year absence. Despite the years, the let-downs, and the strangeness of it all, he returned to Paris with a handful of good memories and a promise from Tomatis to come visit, but a whole year has passed waiting for Tomatis to make travel plans. Certain Sundays, they would speak on the telephone though they never had anything particular to say. As they lived in different hemispheres,

4

high summer for one meant the other had fists of frozen rain beating at his window. And because of the time difference—morning in the city is evening in Paris, and evening in the city is nighttime in Paris—the weather occupied much of their conversation. Until one Sunday in May, less than two months ago, they spoke about the weather a little longer than usual because, despite the difference in season, country, continent, and hemisphere, climatic conditions were identical (a cold, rainy day), and Tomatis announced the good news at last: in early July he would spend several days in Paris.

But that wasn't all. Tomatis went on to say that Marcelo Soldi—*that bearded lad, they'd spent a day taking his father's dinghy out with the boys to visit Washington's daughter, did he remember?*—meant to send him something he'd been preparing over the last few months, and Tomatis, without further explanation, let drop an enigmatic phrase to pique Pichón's interest: "He went to search for Troy and nearly tumbled into Hades." But it must have been in earnest since, perhaps a month later, the parcel arrived: a very long letter and a floppy disk in a medium-sized, self-sticking bubble envelope, which Soldi had further sealed up with clear adhesive tape as a precautionary measure. Soldi had masculinized the word *disquette* and given it an *accent grave*, which, as written, appeared as *el dìsket*. In a passage from the letter, he said: *"Beyond conversations with Tomatis, who can occasionally tax my patience, I've been amusing myself with impromptu jaunts out to the countryside and poking my nose into old papers that, often miraculously, preserve the memories of this place—or of some other place, if one happens to live elsewhere. What's valid for one place is valid for all space, and we know that if the whole contains a part, the part, in its way, contains the whole."*

And elsewhere in the letter: *"I have a certain advantage over the archive's other aficionados: I get along with the elderly. The text I've sent you in the dìsket was entrusted to me by a woman in her nineties who, I believe, never actually read it. Lucky for her, she died, the poor thing, while I was deciphering and transcribing it with the utmost fidelity into a clean copy, so now I won't have to be evasive or lie to her about the contents of these papers; as their owner has no heirs, I have deposited them in the Provincial Archive where they can be consulted now that I've finished the copies. We are terribly interested in your opinion because, contrary to what I think, Tomatis asserts that the document is not an authentic historical text but a work of fiction. But I say—and I've thought about this carefully—what else are the* Annals, *Lavoisier's* Elements of Chemistry, *the Napoleonic Code, the crowds and cities, suns and universe, but fiction?"* And, at the end: *"The manuscript the old woman gave me was untitled, but if I understood certain passages correctly, I believe the author would not have found it unsuitable if we called it* THE CLOUDS."

The envelope arrives in June, the twenty-first, to be exact, at summer's door.

As Pichón is still finishing out the year at the university, between reunions, exams, and colloquia, he's had no time to investigate the contents of the mysterious *disket*, by now covered in dust, abandoned somewhere among the books, notepads, and papers on his desk. On July second, his wife and boys leave for the seaside, and he has remained in Paris, delayed by a couple appointments, and because Tomatis has announced he'll arrive in Madrid at seven that night. The two men have decided to spend two or three days together in Paris where they will be able to speak more freely, and plan to travel together afterward, meeting up with Babette and the children in Brittany.

That morning, around 9:30, Pichón attends a faculty meeting and remains in his office afterward, working until 2:30, when he goes out for ice cream, then heads home for a siesta. Many city-dwellers have already left and, as the tourists (for some reason) have yet to arrive, perhaps preferring the ocean or the mountains in the excessive heat, the city is deserted; because of his family's trip, so too is Pichón's flat, hereby establishing a curious parallel between home and city. As the windows are always open to capture stray currents of air, there exists between the city and house a sort of continuity; for a moment, he can't tell which contains the other. There is a silence, older and grander than usual, and it expands with the coming of hot, sticky night after the interminable day. Pichón leans out the second-story window in his shorts with all the lights off, surveying the quiet, empty street, and smoking cigarette after cigarette, taking in the night as through a stethoscope—not so much the external details as the sensations those details arouse within him, taking him back to the past, to his childhood most of all, to moments so bright and intense that time seems to stop; to the point where he's forced to consider that many sensations he's always believed unique to a place in fact belong to summer.

Around 7:00, a little dazed from the heat and his overly long nap, he leaves to do some shopping in the neighborhood, but after dallying in a wine shop, selecting bottles of white for the coming days, he finds himself feeling refreshed, clean, and perfectly content, passing back through the blue evening air down stifling, deserted streets, and returns to his empty house. As soon as he enters, he goes to shower, dries himself gently, patting the towel on his skin, as one dabs blotting paper over lines of fresh ink, never rubbing; then he puts on only a clean pair of shorts. He has a light dinner—a slice of ham, a few tomatoes, a nugget of cheese, and mineral water—but when he sits down at the computer, starting it up and inserting the *disket* to read out its contents on the screen, he thinks the better of it and makes his way to the refrigerator. He returns with a big, white crockery mug of cherries, sets it on his desk within reach of his left hand, amid the mess of pens, pencils, lighters, and cigarette packs, and an ashtray of heavy, dark green glass. He begins to read the text marching down the screen, and though he lifts the cherries to his mouth, one by one, without

7

looking, the taste, at once sweet and tart, conjures vivid little red globes in his mind as if the flavor and feeling they're about to produce on his tongue make a detour through his eyes, or through memory, before arriving in his brain. Large, meaty, cold, gloriously firm and red, by chance the first he's gotten, the reality is that although they've been flourishing, the month of July is flying by, and, as much as he hopes otherwise, they are the last cherries of summer. And nothing reassures Pichón that once this black, interminable summer has passed, they'll return again with that same capricious grace, emerging from nothing into the light of day.

* * *

Rivers swollen to excess, an unexpected summer, and that
most-peculiar cargo: With the perspective of time and distance,
these three things could sum up our hundred leagues of troubles,
explaining the paradoxical difficulty of crossing the flatlands.

That arduous, protracted voyage took place, as if I could forget, in the August of 1804. On the first of that month, we set out
for Buenos Aires during a terrible freeze, horseshoes cracking at
blades of hoarfrost, a blue-tinged pink in the dawn, but within
a few short days we found ourselves embroiled in a summer as
squalid as it was cruel.

We made progress ten times faster on the trek from Buenos Aires
to the city, Santa Fé, than we did on the return journey, though
there were just four of us on horseback that time, and despite
countless obstacles and the cold always tormenting us, even in full
sunlight. And so this sudden onset of sweltering heat was doubly

confounding, both for its great intensity and for its unseasonable arrival, contradicting the laws of nature and the order of the seasons. How little nature takes our plans into account; she proved insolent, opposing the laws that contain her, with that strange heat in the depths of one of the bleakest winters the region, according to numerous testimonials, had suffered. That unwholesome "summer," which blossomed into a sham spring only to be obliterated a few days later, unleashed an anomalous chain of seasons marching in hurried disarray, all in the space of a month. But Osuna, the man who guided us to the city and who took us, in a large convoy this time, back to Buenos Aires, kept saying that every so often a mid-August dry spell like this would set in, preceding the Santa Rosa storms on the thirtieth. Suffice it to say, he was right as always, and on the thirtieth precisely, some days before we reached our destination, the predicted storm descended to crown our parade of hardships—though it also helped to extricate us from a most precarious situation.

But I am getting ahead of the facts and, perhaps, out of consideration for the possible reader, decades from now, into whose hands this memoir might someday fall, it would behoove me to introduce myself: I am Dr. Real, specialist of those afflictions not of the body, but of the mind and soul. A native of the Bajada Grande of the Paraná, I was born and raised in those treacherous northern hills where the great river's ceaseless red current has its source. I learned my letters under the Franciscans, but when I reached the age for a young man to delve into his studies, my parents thought Madrid preferable to anywhere else as the capital of knowledge; this can be accounted for by the fact that they were Castilian, and hoped the tumult dividing France—a commotion which had shaken Europe for the past six or seven years—would not reach the Universidad de Alcalá de Henares. Unlike my parents, I was drawn to that commotion, and, given my growing interest in diseases of the mind, when I caught wind that Salpetrière Hospital was allowing its madmen off their chains, I resolved to continue my studies amid the frays of Paris rather than the sleepy cloisters of Alcalá. As happens so often throughout history, the final decade of the last century had been tumultuous; like all parents, mine sought to educate me at the edges of that tumult, and, like all young people, I sensed it was within that very tumult where my life was to begin.

And I was not mistaken. I discovered a new science in the Parisian hospitals and, among its principle representatives, Dr. Weiss. A handful of doctors-thinkers asserted, like those ancient philosophers with whom they consorted, that even though there were decisive bodily factors, in true mental disease the cause should be sought not in the body, but in the mind itself. Dr. Weiss had come to Paris from Amsterdam in order to confirm that analysis; I, his junior, upon discovering the existence of the learned Dutchman and his teachings, might even have said the man and his hypothesis formed a single identity. At the time of my arrival, the idea had become a passionately discussed theory, and Dr. Weiss became my friend, teacher, and mentor. So, when he decided to settle in Buenos Aires to practice according to the principles of the new discipline, I naturally became his assistant. It should also be noted that before making his final decision, he questioned me at length about the region and its inhabitants, and as my intention in this memoir is to scrupulously respect the truth in all, I must admit that moving to the Americas had been his aim far longer than he had known me, and that his interest in my insignificant person only grew once he had learned from a third party that I came from Río de la Plata. The faraway Spanish colonies were already attracting scientists, traders, and adventurers; the motherland's stockade, in place to isolate the colonies, was riddled on all sides with holes; it was quite simple to slip in through the gaps, to the point that even those appointed by Madrid to prevent such things profited

11

from the situation. But Dr. Weiss was not the sort of man to involve himself in smuggling. Before crossing the ocean (and, might I add, with greater ease than it took me some years later to cross a sea of solid ground), we petitioned the Court and in a few months obtained the necessary authorization. So it was that in April of 1802, Dr. Weiss's Casa de Salud was unveiled two or three leagues north of Buenos Aires, in a place called Las Tres Acacias, not far from the river but on high terrain to prevent flooding, with the short-lived triple blessing of the prominent locals, the authorities of Río de la Plata, and the Crown. Dr. Weiss's intentions were not philanthropic—for him, growing rich was rather a means to further his investigations and, if possible, recoup part of his initial invest-ment. He had sunk his entire family fortune into books, travel, measures to sway influential people to grant him any necessary authorizations, and, most of all, into the construction and upkeep of the aforementioned Casa de Salud, a vast, multi-winged edifice with thick, white walls and tiled floors on a hill overlooking the river.

The Casa was patterned after a model already existing in Europe, particularily in Paris, where several institutions of this type had been founded in recent years, but the architecture was inspired by the convent or *béguinage*, the philosopher's retreat, vaguely remi-niscent of the Academy and the Garden of Epicurus, rejecting the otherwise typical chains, jail, and dungeon: The result was an ideal hospital for the provision of rest and care which, unfortunately, by its very nature, only the ailing rich would be able to enjoy. But Dr. Weiss intended to look after the poor as well, elsewhere and by other means, for even if the poor proved indifferent (which of course was not the case), his scientific interests demanded it. For him, mental illness was sometimes due to concomitant causes from different parts of the body, but the better part of the ill-nesses began in the mind itself, along with other external causes from the surrounding world: climate, family, status, race, strain. That the rich alone were able to afford treatment offers a sense of its meticulous complexity: Each patient was considered a unique case, treated gently and appropriately over the course of a lengthy regime that required not just time but space, labor, and expertise. Sensible of the fact that rich families did not know what to do with the mad, and that, to protect their reputations, they desired a place to take in their madmen, as they refused to let them wander the streets like the poor did with their own, the doctor had the idea to open his Casa de Salud, providing a surrogate home for what the sick had lost: It was perhaps the first of its kind in all the American territories.

Before its inauguration, the number of applicant families was surprisingly high, and though they were all from Buenos Aires, pleading letters began to arrive from the provinces within a few months of operation—from Paraguay, Peru, and Brazil, each one underscoring the great need in America for a place to treat phrenitis, mania, melancholia, and other more or less familiar mental ailments with the very latest scientific advances. To tell the truth, it was almost as though such diseases did not exist in the American upper classes until Dr. Weiss and I arrived to treat them; one might infer from the silence prevailing across the continent that those infirmities, at least without the existence of a science able to identify them, had been taken to be standard personality traits, which might explain all those incomprehensible deeds in our history. What *is* known is that the Casa was nearly full shortly after opening, and in the following year the doctor began to draw up plans for the construction of a supplementary wing.

This warm reception is easily explained: For those who do not know how to manage them, the mad rarely prove dangerous, but are always tiring. Even when families endure them with goodwill and, above all, lots of patience, at a certain point they exhaust themselves. Trying to make a madman behave like everyone else is like turning the course of a river: I do not mean that it is impossible, but rather that only a good engineer, lacking any prior assurance of his success, can try to set the water running the other way. For the general populace, the madman's outlandish behavior is stubbornness, pure and simple, or even a fabrication. Impervious to common sense and reason, those who insist too much on trying to redeem the mad are the very persons who find their own minds disturbed. Take into account, also, that the stricter the principles of their environment, the more the lunatics' peculiarities will stand out and the more ridiculous their eccentricities will seem. Among the poor, bound by survival to display more tolerant principles, madness seems more natural, as if it contrasts less with the senselessness of their misery. But one of the oldest wishes of the mighty, precisely the one upon which they would base their power, is to embody reason; madness in their midst, then, poses a real problem. A madman endangers a house of rank from ceiling to cellar, costing the occupants their respectability, and so they almost always hide mental illness like a scandal. *There must be many families over there, too, that do not know what to do with their mad,* Dr. Weiss said to me one day in Madrid, as we waited for the Court's authorization to open our house in the Viceroyalty. For the science that makes them its object, the mad are an enigma, but for the families who keep them in their homes, they are nuisances. Obviously, complications arise when the external signs of insanity become too obvious. In the cases that go unnoticed, though, which are far more frequent than one might believe, that same insanity can rise through the ranks by general consensus, to hold the world on a string.

As I realize many of my words today still reflect the influence of my revered teacher, I believe it is advisable to evoke him in greater detail. Of his appearance, suffice to say that at first glance he betrayed himself as a man of science: tall, a little heavy; a deeply receding hairline that left graying blond hair permanently disheveled around a reddened brow. This exposed the ongoing activity within his head, which was rather larger than normal and well situated atop strong shoulders. Bright blue eyes shone behind gold-rimmed glasses, which danced against his chest on a fine gold chain around his neck (when they were not creeping up his nose)—roving and perceptive eyes, slightly ironic, and, in moments of great concentration, they disappeared behind half-closed lids, betraying his mind's utmost occupation. His frank, ruddy face darkened slightly when he examined a patient, but at the dinner hour, after a day of hard work, wine and conversation were his chief pleasures. Nearly ten years after his death, I betray no secret in writing of his passion for the female sex; it was exaggerated even at his advanced age, and, as occurs often in northerners, his predilection was for the darker races. Brothels did not frighten him; on the contrary, they exercised too great a draw, and married women seemed to emanate further and unfathomable charm for his sensual appetites. As I was his principal interlocutor, his assistant, and his faithful disciple, and I found myself so often at his side as to be mistaken for his shadow, I became, for obvious reasons, his confidante. So I consider myself with all clarity of conscience to be the person who, at least in the final third of his life, knew him best. When Casa de Salud no longer stood and, for reasons beyond our control, we had to separate upon our return to Europe, he went back to Amsterdam while I began as an intern at the hospital in Rennes, of which I am currently the deputy director; until the day of his death we continued to write each other, mingling the scientific with the personal in our correspondence with fluency and good cheer. He was scrupulous about hygiene and, when the weather was hot, he liked to dress impeccably in white; on summer nights in Buenos Aires, when he left after dinner to pursue his

15

fondest pastime, it was not uncommon, on seeing him pass by from darkened thresholds, from half-lit bedrooms, through wide-open windows seeking to catch a phantom breeze, to hear a male voice murmur in the darkness, mocking yet understanding, *There goes the blond doctor, looking for whores.* I believe the best way to describe Dr. Weiss is by that capacity he possessed for practicing his vices freely, for all to see, without loss of respectability. This was likely because he never mixed business with pleasure and was a man of his word: I never heard him tell a lie nor promise something he was not prepared to carry out. His immoderate and mysterious love of married women forced him to perform the odd moral balancing act, and on two or three occasions, forced by circumstance into inevitable duplicity, I saw him give up, resignedly, the pleasures he had already been assured. From these proclivities he fashioned a way of life, a discipline of knowledge and of living, almost a metaphysics. In a letter from his final days, he wrote to me: *The moment, esteemed friend, is death, death alone. Sex, wine, and philosophy, they tear us from the moment, they keep us, temporary things, from death.* Although he seemed to make no distinction between healthy and diseased, he treated our patients with the greatest decency, as though he thought he owed them more respect than the sane. And in a way, he was correct: Abandoned by families who rarely came to visit, the madmen were entirely in our hands; to them we represented a last link to the world. Upon the opening of Casa de Salud, Dr. Weiss warned the other staff and me that it was foolishness to lie to the patients, and that the sick would have sniffed us out just as sane people discern when madmen do everything possible to conceal their insanity, not realizing that those very efforts betray them. According to Dr. Weiss, deception is pointless because madness, by mere fact of its existence, renders the truth problematic. A detail that intrigued me when I heard him talk with patients: Often, in the face of the madmen's wildest assertions, he would flash a brief smile of approval, not in his tightened lips, but in his blue eyes.

Illnesses—and not just mental, but physical, which he was capable of treating with equal skill, though which he refrained from so as not to alienate other medical practitioners in the city, unwilling to draw away their clients—were not my teacher's only area of interest: All the most varied manifestations of the natural world aroused the same curiosity in him, stimulating his gifts of reason and observation, from the regular turning of the stars to the tiniest prairie flowers, which he collected in a detailed herbarium. An insect, a mild October breeze, the behavior of horses, or the phases of the moon held equal value for him as objects of reflection, and more than once I heard him say that contrary to what man had made, there was no hierarchy in nature, and the laws that dictate the entire universe are present in every natural phenomenon. So by accurately explaining, for example, a flea-jump—he always liked trivial examples—one might comprehend the operation of the solar system. He also noted that the correct interpretation of a natural fact was in any event impossible, for as knowledge of the world increased, so too did its mysterious dark side.

He was a pleasant, helpful man, or perhaps more than pleasant and helpful: He was given to compassion. That feature of his character was much more commendable in him than in any other. Indeed, it kept him in check, as, in religious matters, I never saw a more avowed atheist. In one of his letters from Amsterdam, he told me: *As God does not exist, it falls to us men to correct the world's flaws. How I would have liked to leave him to that task—at the end of days, if he exists, evil would be his responsibility—and to be able to dedicate all my time to the one perfect thing he is known to have created: the female sex!* His atheism sometimes left me perplexed; he always appeared to think the nonexistence of God an exhilarating condition. Although I shared his beliefs, I must confess that often, in my innermost thoughts, it all seemed rather discouraging, less for the infinite nothingness it attributed to my own being than for the incredible waste, supposing the existence of such a vast universe, varied and colorful, burst open at some time, some fine day, and generously left in our charge, all so it might suddenly collapse and disappear. Such an eventuality left Dr. Weiss unmoved; on the contrary, it seemed to encourage him. I believe that if he were to stand at the mouth of an erupting volcano—a speculation, in any case, though I think he lived in Naples a few years before we met—he would not have fled, but rather rubbed his hands together, preparing to study the igneous material about to consume him. This is an adequate comparison to describe our fourteen years at Casa de Salud. Seething lava threatened us from all sides: Indians, bandits, the English, and the Spanish royalists we called *godos* (in order of increasing ferocity), not to mention storms, floods, droughts, locusts, accusations, lawsuits, wars, and revolutions. Our hospital-laboratory, as the doctor called it, conceived as peaceful and white, ended as a miserable ruin, which, a friend has informed me, still exists today among the weeds. It seems, after the tragic scattering of our boarders—we searched for them for weeks without success—two of them returned the following year and settled in the ruins with no family to claim them. (Until their death, the Indians worshiped them and brought them food each day. Later, my friend learned the Indians were Christian converts from Areco who, in secret, were practicing a sort of cult around the two madmen, whom the Indians treated well so as to gain protection from the forces of evil.)

Politics and money are useful, no doubt, but they distract from what matters: Also distracting were the successive wars and greed of certain families, who paid the first year's costs to cast off their sick and, having entrusted them to the Casa, forgot to continue payment, bringing an end to our venture. As for the authorities,

18

while some enlightened persons encouraged us, many leaders, mostly businessmen, petty lawyers, ranchers, churchmen, and soldiers, nearly all of them eager, obscurantist, and uneducated, watched us constantly and created all manners of interference to our growth. Only those who dealt with Dr. Weiss directly supported us, having experienced his goodness, sincerity, and efficiency in their exchanges. And perhaps because they depended on him and because he had been known to ease their suffering on more than one occasion, the patients idolized him. I can tell you, he was able to speak with even the most violent of patients who thought he held them prisoner without cause and was torturing them, even patients who thought him their enemy and never stopped trying to hurt or threaten him. Despite this, those very men clearly respected him, though perhaps they never realized it, and when they feigned the belief that the doctor was the cause of all their ills, I could see in their words and carriage that they did not truly believe their claims. One way or another, they seemed to want him to give a sign that they were mistaken, or maybe extra attention or special interest, trying to goad him with libelous insults that the doctor bore with his impassive little smile, sometimes coming to nod his head affirmatively as though he approved of them. The workers in the Casa, those he was likewise mentoring—they, too, were devoted to him. For the most part, the doctor dealt with fairly uneducated people, but he believed the attributes his work required—intelligence, gentleness, physical strength, and patience—did not depend on schooling. Some ladies from the city tried to work with the Casa as an act of charity, but, with diplomatic cleverness, the doctor convinced them that it was dangerous work, at least in certain cases, terribly rare, to be sure, and once he managed to rid himself of them, he remarked to me confidentially, with his habitual little smile and a twinkle in his eye, *Though I must say, I wouldn't mind requesting a certain service from the younger ones.*

It was the doctor who conceived and executed plans for the Casa. It consisted of a single, rectangular floor with a series of corridors that enclosed three courtyards. The façade faced the river, *Just as the temple of Concordia faces the sea in the land of Empedocles,* he would joke. The stout adobe walls were always an immaculate white; the trellis beneath the windows suggested colonial mansions, but rows of rooms that opened onto impeccable courtyards evoked the convent, monastery, or a rustic Academy. Only in the last corridor of the last courtyard did the doors have a lock. In the others, including my teacher's, such protection was unnecessary. We lived alongside our mad. As for those working in the Casa, they kept only what they wished, which was very little, under lock and key. The rooms at the far end were reserved for patients who underwent periods of serious volatility. Certain madmen grew accustomed to their constant frenzy, or resigned themselves to it, but the sudden attacks of the silent, gloomy ones were often the most aggressive. In those cases, isolation became necessary, and we left them alone until their melancholia won out again. Strictly speaking, with our method, which is to say, Dr. Weiss's method, over those fourteen years, we rarely faced raving lunatics who might have endangered our community or any of its members. When violence tempted our patients, it was more often against themselves. One of them would sometimes go suddenly running with a *bang* against the wall, for no apparent reason, leaving himself dazed and bloodied. Another, without prior warning, thought to cut himself all over with a knife. But in fourteen years, we mourned only three suicides. A Brazilian boy, ever and irresistibly drawn to water, found his end by casting himself into the river; one old man hung himself from a tree in the second courtyard one winter morning; and one woman poisoned herself. (She had given herself six months to recover, and, as she explained in the letter she left behind, she had arrived at the Casa with the poison hidden

20

and had resolved to use it if the doctor's treatment, her last hope for a cure, should fail.)

The staff, intermingled with the patients, was distributed throughout the three sets of corridors; they actually formed three squares, each with two shared interior sides. Built in a row and all continuous, the three squares aligned to form a rectangle together. The middle square shared two transverse walls with the first square past the entrance and the one farthest off; in matters of architecture, the doctor was fond of geometry. The first of those transverse sides in the middle square was a long salon that served as a refectory with a kitchen at one end. The cook was an employee, but his helpers and serving boys were all mad. Per Dr. Weiss's instructions, when one of them wanted to cook, the chef placed the kitchen at his disposal. In fact, the cook once went to visit his family on the other side of Buenos Aires for two or three days, leaving the kitchen in the hands of a patient. In the lateral corridors opposite the lower square, just past the entrance, Dr. Weiss and I each had our rooms, which also served as our offices, his to the left and mine to the right.

In our Casa de Salud, truth be told, there were very few medicinal remedies. According to Dr. Weiss, of the various causes that might explain insanity, the most improbable were those that came from the body, and he posited that in matters of mental illness, the cause must be sought out in the mind. As the doctor told me in one of his first letters from Amsterdam: *But that mixture of sensations, passions, imagination and thought, truth and lies, good and evil, love and hate, crime and remorse, desire and renunciation that is the mind, does not make our work easier. In a sense, for men the body is a remote region of their very selves, and if they hold it responsible for all their evils, they resign those evils to the control of nature, which for them is synonymous with fate. In what they call the mind, however, they themselves are deeply implicated. In the vast majority of cases, exchange with the outer world does not occur within the body, but in the mind. The body is a hidden land that few are privileged to tread or contemplate, while the mind is in constant exchange in the public square, and those who boast of maintaining a pure, hidden mind fail to see the point: That property they believe to be remote and ethereal, others can sully. For this reason, practically everyone prefers to find the cause of all wrongdoing in the body.*

At any rate, Dr. Weiss's principal method consisted of maintaining identical relations with the patients as he did with the sane, and only in extreme cases did he try some sort of treatment, often temporarily: the prescription of certain medications, for example, or confinement, or hot or cold baths. On rare occasions we found ourselves obliged to use a straitjacket. As for the baths, they were part of our routine, and patients bathed in a separate structure near the river, as white and well kept as the main building. We treated physical ailments by the usual methods, and in more serious cases, the doctor did not hesitate to summon one of his colleagues from Buenos Aires for a consultation. But I must add, if I want to abide by the utmost truth, that the vast majority of the many patients under our care seemed to enjoy exceptional health, physically speaking. Ensconced in their own worlds created entirely by their delirious imaginations and often incomprehensible to the rest of us, they seemed protected from the natural condition endured by those who enjoy, as they say, their full faculties. Encased in their own illusory worlds, the patients seemed to take root, and so did not suffer the decay that befalls all physical substance, but rather an interminable drying-up, a slow calcination whose hardening was not measurable with known instruments. The parts of them that came dislodged—hairs; teeth; skin; the occasional eye that seemed to vanish into thin air from behind a sealed eyelid; a few fingers severed in an accident; a leg that seized up and refused to walk, obliging one to always drag it like an old piece of furniture—these were like shreds of wrapping, torn in the bustle and commotion of a journey without the parcel they protect suffering the slightest damage.

When it came to housework, each helped according to his needs and as desired, and repairs, painting, and the orchard and gardening, along with maintenance of the farmyard (which lay outside the building past the three large acacia trees that gave the place its name), and kitchen tasks as I have already mentioned, were shared as necessity arose among whatever volunteers turned up, Dr. Weiss included. More than once, I saw him tend to a patient as he worked in the garden or painted the adobe walls, the preservation of whose immaculate whiteness, along with the scrupulously clean rooms and corridors and the care of the farmyard and tree-lined courtyards, occupied most of the day's labor. With regard to these communal chores, I ought to note they did not result from disciplinary impositions, but rather from the whim of the patients volunteering; this labor system that Dr. Weiss so carefully devised yet again proved his inimitable realism and unerring shrewdness. If madness is defined by the very delusions it manifests, and if in many cases the patients are free from physical pain, it is clear that its other consistent feature is unruliness: Reason, though capable of imposing its discipline even onto lightning that drops from the sky, is not enough to tame delusion. He who wishes to deal with the lunatic is wiser to appeal to his caprice rather than to his obedience. Our mad did not often follow externally dictated standards, but rather what their own delusion required, sometimes with the fore-seeable consequence that the outer world, hitherto unquestionable, yielded to them. I recall an incident in 1811, when a Revolutionary official whom I would have numbered among our enemies, charged with inspecting our establishment, took an unexpected tumble from his horse during the first days of his visit—though it failed to shuffle him loose the mortal coil, as they say. He commented at

23

the end of his stay, not inappropriately, that during his recovery at the Casa he had spent all his time trying to distinguish the madmen from the sane, to which my esteemed teacher responded—the usual twinkle in his bright blue eyes, but without receiving even the slightest smile of complicity in return—that when he passed through the streets or halls of Buenos Aires, he was frequently assaulted by the same bewilderment.

The object of this memoir is not a detailed relation of life in Casa de Salud, but our voyage of 1804, whose scant hundred leagues were multiplied by obstacles, foreseen or unforeseen, that delayed our advance, and by natural phenomena that upset our plans, and by certain unusual episodes that led us more than once to the brink of disaster. But before I tell the story, I want to remark upon the circumstances that led to the Casa's fall.

In Madrid, we obtained the necessary authorizations to settle with ease, which can be explained by the fact that the Crown believed each new institution founded in the colonies helped to solidify its presence there. It is also explained by the ignorance of nearly all the Court officials regarding our area of expertise and the manner in which we thought to exercise it, even though Dr. Weiss had been partly inspired by the example of some doctors in Valencia who had practiced a more humane treatment of madness during the previous century. To this I might add the fact that we had to pay a tax because, in truth, taking into account the financial state of practically every European monarchy, it always sped proceedings along. Besides, convinced of the nonexistence of anything outside their purview, the dignitaries believed there were no madmen in America with families able to pay for someone to look after them, so in their private counsel they doubtless thought that Dr. Weiss and I were two naïfs, ready and willing to squander his fortune on a half-cocked undertaking destined for failure. But when the long white rectangle opened its doors at the feet of the three acacia trees and the patients began to flock in, local dig-nitaries began to take us seriously and, when word of our novel methods spread, public opinion split over their seriousness, their efficacy, and even their decency. The Church for example, which granted itself power in the colonies of which it would never dare dream in the motherland, sought to judge how patients should be treated, requiring Dr. Weiss's inexhaustible patience and clever-ness, ever-ready to overcome any difficulties. During our private deliberations, the doctor told me that, for the moment, a direct confrontation with the clergy would be unproductive and not with-out danger, and that the best way to fight them was to proceed with our scientific work without making concessions; but, at the same time, even when we ought to have avoided provocation, he was unwilling to renounce his ideas. When the Revolution came years later, we hoped it would also come for us and that our work would finally be recognized, but many of its supporters were no different from its enemies in terms of political, scientific, and reli-gious views. The wars that followed did little more than exacerbate the situation: The civil war was already brewing in the wars for independence, and one might even say that the first battles of the war for independence were in fact a sort of civil war, for those killing each other were the same as those who, five or six years earlier, had been fighting together against the English. Though in truth the region had never really been calm, during wartime we often saw companies of soldiers passing through by land or water, sometimes branching off from their route to come knock at our door out of curiosity or to see a doctor, or sometimes to beg a little water or even something to eat. Most often, when they realized they had found a hospital, and especially when they discovered what kind of patients we treated, they rushed off, leaving us in peace: It is already known that madness often provokes unease, if not laughter, and, more often than not, consternation and fear.

It was not all misunderstandings and threats in the surrounding world, and I must recall that in the fourteen years of Dr. Weiss's Casa de Salud, a group of friends and advocates, hailing from all social classes and political factions—including dignitaries of the successive governments, scientists, and even members of the clergy—backed our expertise in every way. A good part of our madmen's families, if only so they would not have them reappear suddenly in their houses one day if our institution closed, always paid on time, as each without exception formed part of the moneyed classes that, whatever faction they belonged to, were the only ones who granted themselves the right to govern, using their influence however they could to ensure we were not bothered. But on several occasions, grudges, rivalries, and conflicts of interest nearly brought us to ruin. When the wars of independence began, the revolutionaries accused us of being royalists, and the royalists, of being revolutionaries. As the Crown had authorized our settlement, the *criollo* revolutionaries accused us of espionage, and a few even expected us only to admit foreign patients to the Casa from families supporting the Revolutionary cause. The most ridiculous thing about that situation was that Dr. Weiss and I had always been avowed revolutionaries—he had been in the streets of Paris in ninety-three—but as we were forced to conceal this during the Spanish Viceroyalty in order to survive, the revolutionaries claimed we chose to defend their cause out of opportunism or, even worse, in order to more effectively carry out our supposed duty as spies. What followed was what follows in all revolutions, really, which is to say, the leaders were in one small group made up of die-hard revolutionaries, who always lose in the end, while the rest was comprised of one part influential men from the previous government, changing sides as they went along, and one part those neither with nor against them, who simply seek to gain advantage from the unforeseen circumstances that brought them to power. Aside from the families who had entrusted one of their own to us and from certain scientists who were genuinely interested in our work, no one understood what it was we were doing, and so we suffered the eternal scourge that threatens those who think, or those who mistrust a man who denies what he does not understand.

I have been told that these days (*Roughly 1835 by my calculations.* Note, M. Soldi) they go slitting throats all across the land; in my day it was the firing squad that seemed to be the fashion. An unforeseen ally saved us from this painful and, in short, all-too degrading end: the English consul, who considered us—you will pardon me for taking the liberty in my account of attributing to a diplomat, and an Englishman no less, the faculty of thought—a couple of charlatans, even suspected, with just cause on his part, that in reality Dr. Weiss and I, who were often in the habit of crossing him at social gatherings, were having our fill of laughs at his expense. Shortly after resettling in Amsterdam, the doctor wrote to me: *I have arrived here safe and sound again in Europe, and all thanks to Mister Dickson. The poor man, torn between his hatred of Spain (for commercial reasons) and his hatred of all that is revolutionary (his national idiosyncrasy), he finds himself ever the servant of two masters, lacking sympathy for either. And all the same, his sense of honor, lacking any hold on reality, has saved our lives.* I trust I do not offend anyone by explaining, twenty years later, the allusions contained in the doctor's letter.

For several months, a Chilean youth had been interned in the Casa, sick with melancholia, his father having been executed on the charge of high treason in Valparaíso for taking up the Spanish cause. A government spy informed a military officer in Buenos Aires about the Chilean youth's presence at Las Tres Acacias, and the officer held that the doctor and I kept the young man at the Casa on the pretext of his illness to protect him, and that he was not actually sick but was rather a fugitive, which proved, according to the officer, that we were spies for the King of Spain, as some suspected. The young man was seriously ill, seized with the deepest melancholy, and naturally we refused to surrender him. But when the military emissaries withdrew, Dr. Weiss, looking concerned, explained to me that he, like the officer, knew the Chilean youth was no more than a pretext and that the real reason was the officer's unspoken suspicion that his wife was cuckolding him with the doctor: *A libelous suspicion,* sighed the doctor, *for Mercedes and I haven't seen each other for six months.* So it went that my dear teacher's inexplicable taste for married women nearly brought us before the firing squad.

Two or three days later, they arrested us and threatened the staff into departing for their homes. A couple of men, nobly concerned for the patients, who returned secretly to the Casa, were flogged, staked, and forcibly conscripted into the army. The building was brutally and deliberately looted and smashed as the patients fled in terror. The doctor and I were imprisoned in the jealous officer's camp for three weeks until they came for us one day at dawn and, joking and saying they were going to shoot us, brought us out to the countryside; having given us a beating, they mounted us bareback, half-dressed, on a single horse—I had the reins—and set us free.

In Buenos Aires, the doctor sought redress from the government for the officer's unforgivable conduct, and that was how we uncovered a fact more horrible than our adventure: Despite his illness, the Chilean youth had been arrested on the soldier's orders, and was shot the next day on the charge, no less ignominious than it was false, of treason. We were heaved about by anger and pain, staggering between anxiety and revenge, but the most important thing was to search for the patients the marauders had set loose. So with the help of our protectors, we formed a party and went out into the vastness of the plains to find them. Faithful Osuna, untouched by the years, guided us through that feature-less expanse—like him, ever the same—in which he alone was able to perceive the details and nuances. But though we searched day and night for weeks, we did not see a single trace of the patients. Many years later, until the day of his death, in fact, the doctor and I continued to speculate in our letters about possible explanations for this complete and sudden disappearance.

For the first time I saw the doctor's features reflect a passion previously unknown in him: hatred, and a feeling that saddened me all the more: remorse. Some days, he wandered, somber and silent, amid the wild disorder that the marauding soldiers had left in the Casa: the trampled orchard and garden, plants torn up by the roots, broken glass, furniture hacked into pieces, scorched books with the pages ripped out, papers everywhere. The most fruitful years of our lives had just been senselessly laid to waste by the savagery that, to hide its unspeakable instincts, thought to call itself law and order. Of the boarders we took in at the white Casa of Dr. Weiss, it must also be noted that, even when their own families had disowned them, none of the patients, abandoned by reason and all as they were, took part in these shameful acts. Perhaps this proves an argument I had heard the doctor make to himself many times: Reason does not always express the best of humanity.

We slept in the ruins that night, and the following day we reset-tled in Buenos Aires with what we were able to salvage from the disaster: some books, five or six pages of an herbarium, the bust of Galen which by some miracle had remained intact. But the doc-tor's bottomless sorrow, though it seemed to intensify, did not last for long; three or four days later a new determination, so intense it inspired a little dread in me, appeared on his face. When he decided to put this determination into practice, a grim but solemn spark of satisfaction arose in his gaze. In the back of a tavern one night, inspired by the wine, he explained his plan to me: He would challenge the officer to a duel. The doctor explained his crazy idea, which was essentially a suicide mission, with his customary logical clarity, and was so pleased with the rational evidence that he seemed to have forgotten his many years of medical practice, during which his principal task had been to patiently and insightfully dismantle the hallucinatory fallacies of the patients—patients who were, just as the doctor was now, incapable of seeing for themselves their preposterous concatenations. According to the doctor, the officer would not pursue us, which no doubt was true, and we had no alternatives but flight or confrontation. Yet it was clear we could not go searching for him in his encampment, where his troops' superior numbers were an insurmountable obstacle, nor could we kill him in the street, nor report him to the authorities, which he was a part of and over whom he held considerable sway. Nor were we able to lay an ambush (I am merely listing the options, each one more absurd than the last, that the doctor was proposing). According to him, offending the officer before witnesses and forcing him to fight a duel provided two fundamental advantages: First, the incident would spread word of the officer's barbarity, the Casa's destruction, the shooting of the Chilean youth, and dispersal of the patients, to the public and even to the entire civilized world, and, second (this he voiced with the slightly childish pride of one who has just constructed a flawless syllogism), dueling was the only option that allowed a distant hope of escaping the venture with our lives. At the same time, the provocation would set all responsibility on his shoulders, leaving me free from reprisal. (This gentle concern for my safety was of course a tacit confession of the entire conflict's wanton origins.)

The suicidal plan he had just revealed seemed so unassailable to the doctor that, rubbing his hands together, he told me with his usual lack of hypocrisy that a stroll to the brothel would ease his mind, and he left me in the dark and muddy street, terrified of what was to come. Flight seemed to me, without the slightest doubt, the most sensible of solutions. It is true that the doctor was not one of those who, on the pretext of study, neglected to maintain his body, but he was not a young man either, and further, his adversary, as an officer, was a true instrument of death. There was no mistaking the outcome of that unequal match. But the satisfied glint in Dr. Weiss's gaze robbed me of any inclination to dissuade him.

Ideas as wild as his began to hound me. Nothing stimulates delirium more than being faced with a situation for which one is unprepared; unfathomable as the minuet for the savage or waste for the miser, so were tyrannical power and violence for us, men of libraries and lecture halls. It occurred to me that I could run ahead of the doctor and goad the officer into a duel myself, where my youth might accord me a greater prospect of victory; even if it were to cost me my life, to this very day I am certain that no one would have been able to prevent my teacher, in turn, from provoking that source of all our woes, and that my sacrifice would have been in vain. Convincing him to flee would surely have been an exhausting endeavor, but, more importantly, a useless one: Only one such as me, who knows the elegant adaptability of the doctor's mind, might distinguish his determination from mere pigheadedness. Once he made a decision it was unlikely, if not impossible, for anyone or anything to stop him from setting it in motion. Feeling my way through the muddy streets of Buenos Aires, many solutions, just as half-formed and impossible, struck me and seemed workable for a few seconds until they revealed their absurdity and, with the same fervor that my mind had fleetingly built them, they crumbled. Only when I retired to the peace of my room and, more importantly, to a horizontal position, and the weariness of the day began to fade, did my ideas become clearer, allowing me to conceive of the solution that, as the least fantastical, was the most sensible: going to talk to the officer's wife.

Naturally, if I did so, I would not be able to reveal that I was aware of her relations with the doctor, and I would speak in the name of science, of the tormented patients, appealing to her Christian charity, et cetera. Dr. Weiss could not learn of my interference for anything in the world, as that would hinder the realization of my plan. A few months later, I would write to him in Amsterdam from Rennes recounting my intervention (I lacked the courage to do it during our voyage across the Atlantic) but, to my surprise, he replied that he knew of everything, that a recent missive from Mercedes, having arrived in his hands through none other than the English secret service, contained the explanations I gave in my letter, and some others as will be dealt with later.

After making the necessary inquiries, I sent the officer's wife a discreet message. For two days, I awaited her response, fearing that marauding soldiers would burst into the pension where we were staying to drag us before the firing squad, but on the morning of the third day a negro servant delivered an invitation to a cup of chocolate at an estate on the outskirts of the city. A slave came that same afternoon at five on the dot to guide me to the meeting place.

In a garden, the masters of the house—faultless patriots, as I discovered upon arriving—confirmed what I had already guessed during the first minutes of conversation, namely, that they were relatives of one of our missing patients, who, even as we spoke, might have already died on the plains. When the officer's wife arrived, they tarried with us briefly to exchange a few courtesies after the introductions, but withdrew after a few minutes with the utmost tact. Señora Mercedes listened with hooded eyes as I explained the situation, and I did not refrain from studying her so as to confirm the extent to which her person fulfilled the many feminine attributes that Dr. Weiss preferred: She had a generous figure, poise and self-control, lustrous black hair, and, most importantly, that dark, firm skin which had caused Dr. Weiss to lose his head so many times—even a glimpse of it was always a bewitchment for my teacher: It had the intolerable and delicious strangeness of belonging to another, which was a source of excitement and also of dangerous complications. Time and time again those traits, assembled within a soft, warm body, magnetically drew his energy by some ancient and inexplicable affinity and, with the iron regularity of the constellations, made him orbit their center. When I finished relating the facts, her eyelids rose and her eyes, huge and dark, fixed on mine, revealing so eloquently the intimate thrill of an intense passion and pride that, out of delicacy or prudence, I do not know which, I had to avert my gaze. Señora Mercedes vehemently affirmed that Dr. Weiss's life was more precious to her than her own, and told me she would do whatever was necessary to protect it.

For the first and only time in more than three decades of our friendship, I faced the sad duty of lying to my dear teacher, finding myself in the deplorable situation of a physician who, in concealing the severity of an illness, must hide the truth from an old and dear friend. On the other hand, the meeting with Señora Mercedes, despite the determined air with which she pledged to take the reins on this matter, was unable to reassure me, since I heard nothing more from her. The doctor, as he awaited the occasion to publicly offend our enemy and force him into a duel, went to practice his aim in the field every morning, and then took fencing classes in order to perfect his skills, nonexistent though they were, in that activity. If the destruction of the Casa and the scattering of the patients, the execution of the Chilean youth, and our imminent physical destruction had not grown so serious and tragic, I would have laughed at the situation, which was more than ridiculous.

Only the hours we spent in study calmed us: Closed up in our respective rooms, the candlelight, at times accompanying us until dawn with its flickering brightness, made a paltry halo around visible objects that, for the hours of our quiet contemplation, seemed to hold back the massive shadow outside where so many confusing emotions and so many unhappily-certain threats were creeping.

At last the dénouement: We were invited to a party attended "by all of Buenos Aires," that is, by the members of the revolutionary government and other authorities, officers, clergymen, et cetera; the rich who, as I said before, were more or less the same as those authorities already cited; and foreign diplomats, the French, English, and North Americans especially. Owing to the many factions in open or covert power-struggles, we were also invited despite our recent disgrace. Several government officials, wealthy merchants, and other illustrious intellectuals were on our side for scientific and political reasons, and, in certain cases, even for private reasons, as the doctor had attended to several members of their families years before in Casa de Salud. (Unfortunately, at the time of the Casa's destruction, none of our boarders came from Buenos Aires families; in just two or three cases, we had treated distant relatives.)

Even if, as I believe I have said, Dr. Weiss was naturally careful in his dress, that day his care was multiplied. He spent hours smartening up, as if he thought himself the guest of honor at that assembly, or as if he were attending his own wedding, his own apotheosis, or even, I thought with horror, his own funeral. All that time, I tried in vain to dissuade him from going to the party, until the good-natured disapproval in his eyes forced me to accept, silently, what was to come.

It was a fine party indeed. As it was quite hot, the house was opened up, and several tables were strewn throughout the interior and the garden, where a large canopy had been erected in case of a storm. Lamps shone in the garden, but the rooms gleamed with exceptional lighting that spilled onto the courtyards from open doors and windows. An orchestra sounded, or rather, screeched, a fashionable dance, and couples swayed together across the garden lawn and in illuminated rooms. As two-story houses are quite scarce in Buenos Aires, everything was more or less at ground level, flush with the immense plain on whose eastern border the city is crowded, at the wide and wild riverbanks. Entering the party and cutting across the floor, I had the strange impression that the house, its inhabitants and guests, and the shadowy city that surrounded them, were like a mere morsel in the jaws of an infinite mouth, the black, damp river and vast plains, the boundless firmament—a morsel nestled in a dark and eager cavity, ready to be devoured. That strange idea momentarily distracted me from the critical situation we found ourselves in, but seeing Dr. Weiss, I realized that no consideration, romantic as it was, could divert him from the object he had set upon, and it was hard to tell if it was vengeance or suicide.

Nothing important ever really happens—birth, death, and daily life are colorless and dull—but when something truly strange takes place, it seems less than a hallucination, passing fine and distant as a vague dream. As Dr. Weiss did not see our enemy in the garden, despite his scrutinizing the faces of everyone there with his lively, blue gaze, he headed for the house, my anxious and modest person at his heels. The officer was not in the anteroom, but when we passed through the doorway to the main hall, we discovered him opposite the entryway, beneath a great, gold-framed mirror that hung on the wall, where he conversed in a little group that also included Señora Mercedes. We stopped so suddenly that a few guests by the door looked at us with curiosity: The doctor's blue eyes locked onto the officer's, who, alerted by a fierce animal instinct of which men are deprived, had raised his head when we entered the hall and recognized us straight away. Despite the gravity of the moment, something small distracted me: At his side, Señora Mercedes continued speaking as if nothing had happened, smiling, worldly and fickle, not even lifting her head, though to this day I am convinced that of all the people at the event, she was the first to notice our presence. On the officer's face, surprise gave way to a kind of savage joy, delighting at the thought of wicked deeds that, without his having actually desired them, we were giving him the opportunity to commit. I believe he grasped the situation at once and, seeing us walk decisively toward him, he prepared to receive us as he believed we deserved. As we approached him, I began to acquire the steely conviction that, at the other end of the hall, where the couples dancing made off to one side with astonishment and concern to let us pass, our haphazard lives would come to an end when, suddenly and again, with a funny, dreamlike unreality, the unexpected: Dickson, the English consul, intercepted us, obliging us to stop, and whispered that he had something urgent to tell us on behalf of Señora Mercedes, and when Dr. Weiss refused to listen, Dickson clutched at his jacket and said softly, but with uncharacteristic vehemence, that the message he carried would lead to a better realization of the doctor's plot, and that if we intended to carry it out as planned, we were doomed to failure because we were being ambushed. I felt sweat run down my face, neck, and back, and seeing the large drops that broke out on Dickson's forehead and ran down the creases of his reddened, prematurely wrinkled face, I could imagine, comparing it with the cause of my own sweat, what his frame of mind might be at that moment. The doctor hesitated for a moment, then accepted, and Dickson and I led him from the house. Before we left, I cast a fleeting glance in the officer's direction and saw the disappointment on his face. But when I warily eyed Señora Mercedes, seeing her for the last time in my life before turning away, I confirmed that she

36

had not for a single instant interrupted the cheerful conversation with her interlocutors who, I am sure, had not noticed a thing.

When we left for the garden, not a breeze was stirring in the sultry night, but a feeling of coolness, probably imagined, came over me. Dickson asked that we accompany him to the harbor, where Señora Mercedes's slave awaited us with a message from her lady. We traversed the deserted streets, feeling our way through the dark city amid clouds of buzzing mosquitoes. In a lighted window, behind the grillwork, a man stripped to the waist was eating a piece of watermelon shaped like a half moon. Looking up, he recognized us and, with a sarcasm both gentle and familiar, asked: *Out to see the whores, Doctor?* Whereupon, with his venerable bonhomie, my dear teacher stopped and burst into laughter, which seemed to perturb Dickson, and launched back this unforgettable response: *Not necessarily.* The man shook his head as he took a bite of the watermelon, as if we had lost his interest, and when we resumed our march, despite the gravity of the situation, the doctor's suppressed chuckling echoed in the darkness, irresistibly contagious, so when we arrived at the harbor, our top hats shook against the faint evening light that seemed to diffuse the great open space of the river, whose unmistakable odor, rhythmic splashing on the banks, and genuine coolness in the air betrayed its proximity. Dickson, who retained his seriousness in spite of our certainly unjustified good mood, ordered us to wait and remain silent, and once we obeyed, he began to whistle to notify someone of our presence. Shortly, some thirty meters out, a light signaled and we walked in its direction. When we arrived, six or seven men began to converse in whispered English with Dickson; we were all crammed together around the lantern, studying one another with suspicion and curiosity until the consul, signaling to the doctor and me, moved a few steps away and withdrew into the night. Suddenly, utter darkness overwhelmed me; it took barely a fraction of a second to realize that a cloth had been thrown over my head—a sack, perhaps—and that two or three men had tied my hands. The muffled protests and gasps from the doctor indicated to me, in that total darkness in which I was plunged, that exactly the same thing had happened to him. I tried to struggle, but it was useless. Two powerful arms—Scottish, I discovered later—lifted me up, and it was in that precise moment that my feet ceased to tread the soil of my fatherland forever, or in any case, to this day.

In the letter he sent me from Amsterdam some time later, the doctor offered several additional explanations, since we had already been given the primary ones on the high seas, about what had happened, clarifying the exact motives of the English consul's intervention: *From the outcome of our adventure, one can judge, dear Dr. Real, Señora Mercedes' subtlety and discretion, two attributes we must add to the undeniable charms she possesses and that you, I believe, have had some occasion to admire* de visu. *The explanation for the conduct of Dickson, to whom we were always so unkind, is the following: Some time after we parted, Mercedes, trying vainly, according to her, to forget me, began to visit the English consul, who, without elaborating on what she affirms in her letter, was of course never aware of our relations. Mercedes convinced Dickson that her husband, believing himself cuckolded, had the wrong target, and was going to avenge himself on us, believing I was his wife's lover. Dickson then found himself obliged to intervene. So that's how they saved our lives, the diplomatic service, secret agents, and naval forces of the great island nation that holds the undisputed mastery of the seas, propagating freedom of commerce, as others do the Black Death, wherever they go.*

Hooded by sacks and suffocating, arms bound to our chests by ropes, we were placed on a vessel; the regular sound of its oars accompanied us for some twenty minutes, and then we were hoisted like bundles onto a ship's deck; finally, they removed the sacks, but returned to bind us at the wrists and ankles with our arms behind us—a humiliating treatment that, I recognize, was effected firmly but not roughly—and left us alone in a silent cabin enveloped in the deepest darkness. Distant voices and sounds reached us, and at last we realized that the ship where we lay sequestered had weighed anchor and was sailing at a steady clip to destinations unknown. In the hours of our imprisonment, the doctor, who had not lost the habit or capacity of reasoning with methodical patience, elaborated a series of hypotheses about the remarkable events that had transpired, and when we heard the door open and a man's calm, educated voice began to apologize in English for how they had been obliged to treat us, the doctor (a revealing detail if one takes into account that he had been tied hand and foot and hurled into darkness) responded with perfect tranquility in perfect English that we understood (also perfectly) what had happened, and that we were grateful how quickly the English government had acted to save our lives. When the lights came on we realized we were in the elegant guest cabin of an English frigate, whose captain, a tanned and affable Scotsman, was waiting for the two sailors who accompanied him to untie our bonds and help us to our feet before giving us a jovial welcome. A month later, penniless and still a little shaken, more by recent events than by the volatility of the rough, gray ocean, and the captain having conceded to Dr. Weiss every game of chess they played during the voyage, we disembarked one sad and rainy morning in Liverpool.

I have dwelt on the establishment of Casa de Salud and, in brief, I have noted the treatment methods of Dr. Weiss, his character and philosophy, as well as the ravages of the barbarity that in a few hours left the work not even of years, but of my teacher's entire life, in ruins. It was a calling to build that institution from nothing, especially in a time of unrest, and my sole, original contribution to it was that month-long trip through the plains, in such demanding conditions, which constitutes the principal theme of this memoir.

(In any case, that trip was a unique experience for me, for which, as will be addressed later on, I am also in debt to Dr. Weiss, and I hope that my instructor, forgiving the egoism in supposing to present myself as the protagonist of my tale, will be good enough to consider that I relate what was for me the most singular adventure of my life.)

The patients we had to transfer from the city of Santa Fé, located on the banks of the great river across from my birthplace and some hundred leagues north of Las Tres Acacias, were people disturbed in their innermost selves by the ravages of insanity and required special care; the voyage across the desert plain was an aggravation to their conditions, but their derangement was at the same time itself disruptive, and, by its singular presence, helped break the balance of the old, unwritten laws of the desert. Patients, Indians, women of ill repute, gauchos, soldiers, and even animals, domestic and otherwise—we had to live together for many days in the desert which, though already hostile by definition, saw its hostility increase as unforeseen calamities amassed.

But it is better to start from the beginning. For the most part in the time of the Viceroyalty, when a family wished to place one of its members in Casa de Salud, the transfer of the patient took place independently, and the necessary agreements were carried out by messenger: Over a couple of months, all the details were arranged, and the patient was delivered to us, so to speak, at the door of our establishment, which, once crossed, left him in our hands and as our full responsibility. Such was the unbending rule that governed their hospitalization. Early in 1804, however, four simultaneous requests for admission came to us from different regions, and after laborious negotiations, less of a financial than a practical nature, we consented to gather the patients in the city where I, as Dr. Weiss had decided, would go to fetch them, as said city lay approximately halfway between the places those patients came from and Las Tres Acacias. No expense was too great and no effort was spared when one sought to rid oneself of a madman, as it is difficult to find anything in the world that can be more of a bother, and so with the combined forces of the four families, one of which was in fact a religious community, it was possible to organize a mobile hospital of which I would be a sort of director for the duration of the trip through the desert. (A relative "desert," moreover, for a series of outposts was placed every ten to fifteen leagues or so, and though miserable at best, they alleviated the distance somewhat. Unfortunately, circumstances would deprive us of them.)

That curious convoy we formed and the episodes that arose along our route, in my opinion, deserve a detailed retelling, and if I refrain from publishing it for now, this memoir will provide for some future reader, I hope, not only a picturesque charm, but also genuine scientific interest. Indeed, it is this scientific aspect that prevents the immediate publication of these pages, as my scrupulous preoccupation with accuracy has resulted in notes on the behavior of the deranged and of the other members of the caravan, alongside the transcription of their language, free of empty rhetoric, which might shock certain sensitive souls—but the scientific spirit will not be shocked, for it understands the reality of insanity and the true motivations of both man and beast, and how false by comparison are those notions that pass for rational and prevail in worldly assemblies. Those faithful descriptions, whose absence in a scientific tract would be reproached, might seem offensive in a memoir where personal experiences appear as well, but in this fidelity to truth, indifferent to prejudice and the disapproval of the majority, I do no more than follow the example of Dr. Weiss, who made that fidelity at all times a principle of science, and of life.

So we left at daybreak one morning in June: our guide Osuna, two escort soldiers, and I—still entangled in an anxious night's sleep, teeth chattering with cold as in certain mornings of my childhood—I, who could not manage to hold my horse at a steady gallop to keep pace with my traveling companions. Always riding slightly ahead of us, swathed in his red-and-green-striped poncho, rode Osuna, rigid in his saddle, maintaining his horse's regular stride without any visible motion to denote his mastery over the animal. Of the many hardships that made up our voyage, that image, though of no particular moment, neutral, as it were, is the one that visits me most frequently thirty years later, sharp and vivid: Osuna galloping parallel to the rising sun as it rose from the riverbank, the rider's right side haloed in red while the horse's left profile remained ever blotted with shadow. That image is both more and less than a memory now that, without my willing, returns with its original clarity in the most unexpected moments and situations of the day, and, on certain nights, when I lie in darkness with my head resting on the pillow before sleep's black curtain closes completely, it is the last thing I see; certain mornings, after having deserted me for so long that I have all but forgotten, it is the first thing that appears with such renewed force—I might say it draws all the universe along behind it, making it dance about day-long in the waking theater. (The persistence of this primordial image, the first thing I saw in the light of day to begin my voyage, is explained by the state of elation I found myself in, from Dr. Weiss's trust in me, placing the patients' fates in my hands. Later, I would learn that the doctor had done so knowingly, deliberately. The ordeals of the trip failed to diminish the elation of the departure, whereas caution frequently tempered my enthusiasm at many points during our return.)

Sometimes, straying a little to the east, we drew near the river, and sometimes it was the river that drew near to us. The winter floods were visible in the unusual breadth of the riverbeds and the southerly current, dragging islands of lily pads and logs, branches and drowned animals. From time to time a watercraft struggled upriver, or a raft loaded with goods, shoving off from the bank where it had been moored for the night, was steered by its crew into the middle of the river to be dragged along by the current. The cold remained even in full sun, and by mid-morning we could still feel the horses' hooves crack through the frost and blades of graying pasture-grass, glassy with cold. To the west each morning, and even several days after we had arrived close to our destination a hundred leagues north, the empty fields were dusted with a white layer of frost until almost midday. Twice, we slept out in the open or, rather, tried to sleep, crammed around a meager fire that seemed to smother in the freezing night air, and after a few hours, when it seemed the horses had rested enough, stiff, numb, and drowsy, we took up our march once more. In the darkness of night, the cold-clotted stars did not even twinkle and the icy firmament encircled us, so sudden and crushing that one night I had the unmistakable impression that we inhabited one of its remotest, most insignificant, and ephemeral corners. Dawn had just broken, the air a blue-tinged rose that seemed to trap us in a glacial half-light, a sensation that increased the countryside's soporific monotony, but the sun, already high, turned everything crystalline—sharp, shining, and a little unreal out to the horizon which, no matter how we rode, always seemed fixed in the same place. That horizon so many think of as a paradigm for the outer world—it is no more than a shifting illusion of our senses.

As we encountered the little rivers that flowed west into the Paraná, a lone prospect tormented me, though of course I tried not to discredit myself or to let it show: the possibility that the ferrymen who carried travelers from bank to bank might be missing, and that I would have to swim across, or perhaps use one of those unwieldy leather flotation balls, getting jolted about at the slightest movement. But when some of the rivers were without ferrymen, there were rafts in their place, and of the outposts where we spent the night, only two were close to the water. Of those outposts, only one was a real shelter, uncomfortable to be sure, but at least it was equipped with a clean mess hall, large and sturdy, as the others were little more than ruins, certainly dirtier and more run down. A caretaker in one of them was sick with drink, and we had had to shake him a few times to alert him to our presence, which apparently roused him a little and gave him enough energy to get to his feet. The alcohol, which had already burned through his insides, was eating away at his outsides too; he was the sort of drunkard who always appeared to be living in a state of terror, spending all his time watching the door and starting at every sound, and three or four times in the space of an hour he even left the mess hall to scan the horizon; later, with the first swigs of liquor that loosened the tongue of the otherwise laconic Osuna, the guide explained that the caretaker, utterly alone in the dead center of the countryside, was afraid of an Indian attack.

The following day in the large outpost, eating a nice roast the caretaker had prepared in the courtyard, conversation turned from the cold and encroaching winter, which already threatened all the outposts along the length of the river, to chief Josesito, a Mocoví Indian who had rebelled some time ago with a band of warriors and had attacked outposts, towns, and caravans. The people at the outpost and the travelers who spent the night there knew many stories about the chief, though it was hard to tell if they were true or were just legends attributed to him. After hearing a number of anecdotes, one of the soldiers escorting us declared, with a kind of alcohol-fueled pride, that he had known Josesito in the Barrancas, before the chief turned violent, and that three years earlier, when a company of soldiers had escorted a few friars and some families to Córdoba, Josesito, at that time a fervent Christian living in a reservation south of San Javier, was part of the guard. According to the soldier, whose coarse, somewhat confusing language I translate here to a clearer and more coherent idiom, it was because of a sort of religious dispute that Josesito had deserted civilization, declaring war on the Christians. Osuna, who, at times like these, failed to see when someone had interrupted him and, more importantly, when that person had become the center of attention at his expense, persisted in disagreeing, shaking his head as the other spoke, and when he finally got a word in, he agreed that Josesito, whom he had crossed several times, was in the habit of siding with and later fighting against the Christians out of self-interest and that he, Osuna, aside from horses, white women, and liquor, had no other religion. As he rolled a cigar from one corner of his mouth to the other, its tip emerging from his white and well-trimmed beard (clean enough, too, taking regional customs into account), the caretaker interjected, saying the chief was brave and, as I thought I understood him say, somewhat irritable and erratic, that since childhood he had been quite sensitive to the Christians' arrogance, and that he was one of those who got offended by the smallest word or gesture he thought out of place. As I deduced from the caretaker's words, the simple fact that those Christians existed was already humiliating to the chief: By their very nature, white men held contempt for all who were not like them, as Josesito saw it. He, the caretaker, had known him almost since birth because the boy's father, chief Cristóbal, who was meek indeed and had wanted Josesito educated by priests, used to frequent the mercantile outpost and would bring the boy with him. But since boyhood, Josesito wanted nothing to do with white men. Already at thirteen or fourteen, if, when bartering, some white man made an allusion to his person or treated him in a way he found discourteous, Josesito would shoot him a murderous look. He would not tolerate the smallest familiarity and, of course, was afraid of nothing and no one. Once grown—the caretaker had known him about thirty years—he turned ill-tempered, sullen, and when, in the caretaker's own words, *he'd been at the moonshine,* he could be brutal, itching for a fight. But he was intelligent, and peaceful with those he was fond of. As he had voluntarily placed himself at the margins of society, and as his bad temper was legendary, people attributed all the cruelties of the insurgent Indians, deserters, and outlaws to him. He had learned to play the violin with the priests, and although he vanished from the reservation at fifteen or sixteen upon his father's death, returning to the desert to live by the old Indian ways, and although he would later return with the white men and then go back to the desert many times over, he never once parted with his instrument—he had fashioned a leather strap on the side of his saddle for it, and when riding bareback he wore it slung across his shoulder. After the roast, the bottle of liquor passed from hand to hand as we talked, seated in the hut around a huge brazier, and huddled under two or three ponchos whose folds occasionally revealed pairs of callused, chilblain-roughened hands that stretched, palms down, over the coals. When the caretaker trailed off, for a few seconds no one, not even Osuna, spoke up, and that prolonged and slightly unnerving silence seemed to have an explanation that escaped me—but when someone broke it at last, I understood that everyone there, save me, thought the caretaker had depicted Josesito too favorably for some reason. When I commented on this the next day, just as we were getting underway, Osuna, laconic once more thanks to three or four hours of drunken sleep, suggested in the most elliptical and sphinxlike way that the caretaker had to do business with the chief and was therefore defending him. The night before, when the caretaker had caused that silence and we all remained a little awkward in the sad and paltry lantern light, the audience's disagreement with what we had just heard became apparent when one of those present began to speak, a traveler wrapped in a gray poncho whose eyes, perhaps reflecting the coals, blazed beneath the brim of a black hat worn midway down his brow. Almost motionless by the fire, as if his grossly thick body, layered in garments to protect him from the cold, was a denser region of shadow the lanterns could not dissipate, only his mouth and the bushy black moustache covering his upper lip, flanking the corners, curved and twitched, and while not explicitly contradicting the caretaker, perhaps out of courtesy— after all, even if in exchange for money, the caretaker had shown him hospitality—or maybe out of mere shyness, as if referring to another person and not the same Indian the caretaker had just described, he began telling story after story of the chief Josesito which, if they did follow the general fashion of all the caretaker had said of his temperament, they belied, in contrast, his supposedly peaceful behavior. It is true there are certain ranches, certain caravans, and certain outposts that the chief's band did not attack, said the man, though that offered no proof of goodwill or compassion, but was rather a purely tactical calculation tied to his movements of attack and to his illusory plans meant to throw off the authorities, and to his need for supplies. If he did not burn certain ranches and certain outposts, it was because they stocked him up small-scale on his raids, and at the same time he could use them to make appearances and, in this way, lend himself a peaceful image. But three or four lucky ones, who had miraculously escaped and were the only survivors of his countless and vile bloodbaths, had seen him lead the attacks, recognizing him just by the violin case strapped to his back. One of the survivors was a musician—a circumstance that happened to save his life, but that cost him eight months in captivity—who escaped by sheer chance and told the authorities that, after a massacre, Josesito would walk among the smoking ruins and still-warm, mutilated bodies, playing the violin. According to the musician, said the man, Josesito played very well and had a most expansive repertoire, which he had learned from

47

priests on the reservation, and that, along with the violin, he had memorized a good number of musical scores. According to the man, the musician's tale confirmed what the caretaker had said, namely that he was a sensitive, sullen, tormented Indian. He was rarely heard to laugh, and even with his warriors, who idolized him nonetheless and would have set off into death for him without hesitation, he was mistrustful and distant. According to the man, the chief was passing strange, and the musician had told him that one night, drunk, Josesito had begun threatening him and talking disdainfully of Christian music, making as if to throw the scores into the fire and smash the violin to pieces. The man said that, according to the musician, it looked as though what infuriated the Indian was not that the Christians' music was as bad as he claimed, or that it enjoyed an undeserved reputation, but rather that it was good and that he, Josesito, enjoyed it so, which humiliated him like a vice or weakness.

Shortly thereafter, we laid down to sleep as close as possible to the brazier in makeshift beds on the well-swept floor of the mess hall, where the intense, dry cold set in and, as I found in the morning, froze the ground a glossy blue. Before I lay down, I stepped out into the crisp night air to rid myself of the effects of the liquor that, out of politeness, I had been unable to reject. The moon was round and bright, whiting out the plain, creating a perfect illusion of continuity between earth and sky; pale and abundant light produced a shadow both gray and luminous and the few things set in place by human hands—a tree, a well, the horizontal logs, irregular and parallel to the corral, things that disturbed the empty space—seemed to take on a different consistency than usual in that illusion of continuity, as if the atoms that composed things, according to the illustrious Greek scholar and the meticulous Latin poet, my teacher's teachers and therefore mine, had lost cohesion, betraying the conditional nature not only of their properties, but also of all my notions about them and even about my own self. Sharp as their outlines might appear in the light of day, well shaped and solid in the clear air, they now became porous and unstable, disturbed by a pale, tingling unease that seemed to expose the irresistible force that dispersed substance and mixed it, reducing it to its barest expression, with that gray and intangible flux that mingled earth and sky. A commotion drew me out of my reverie: The horses were stirring in the corral, perhaps alarmed by my presence, but when I took a few steps to block the cold air blowing in their direction I saw I was of no importance to them, for the brief murmur they had made not only failed to increase, but seemed to subside as I drew closer. I remained motionless near them for a time, trying to keep silent so as not to alarm them, examining the silver shadow to which my eyes adjusted bit by bit, and I could see that what had made them shift from time to time, lightly blowing and causing a muted shuffling of indecisive hooves, was their attempt to press against one another for warmth, forming a dark and anonymous mass of breath, flesh, and heartbeat, not so different in the end from how the horsemen had massed around the brazier earlier, joined by the same injustice that forced us to exist without cause, fragile and mortal, under the icy and inexplicable moon.

The following day at dusk, we finally arrived in the city. Not a cloud accompanied us in the sky's pale blue on our last day of travel, but as we arrived, a few slender wisps to the east, motionless against the enormous red disc of the sun as it sunk into the horizon, began to change color: yellow at first, orange, red, violet, and blue, until, having crossed the fork where the Salado river divides and churns into the Paraná, we reached the first miserable hovels on the outskirts, and the air was black from the unrisen moon; under the eaves or within the hovels, the first lanterns began to glow. After coming along with me to the house where I would be staying, which we found without difficulty as its masters were one of the city's leading families, Osuna and the soldiers went off to the barracks where room and board had been arranged for them for the duration of our stay. The Parra family expected me without knowing the exact day of my arrival, and I must say that the welcome they gave me, though they knew I would remain in their house for some weeks, was of the most pleasant sort, perhaps due to the relief of knowing that I came to take their eldest child, who had fallen into a stupor months ago, for treatment at Las Tres Acacias. As it was already nighttime when I arrived, the young man was asleep, and I postponed the examination until the next day; after dinner and a thorough questioning by the others about the news I might have brought from Buenos Aires and even the Court, they took me at last to a clean, orderly room where they had prepared a comfortable bed. Before I went to sleep, I meditated on what undemanding and effusive hospitality they offered me, which was to make my entire stay most agreeable, and I realized that the tedium of life in a country house, lost at the world's edge, must be one of the principal causes.

The next morning, I rose quite early, happy to know that hours of riding did not await me and, as the masters of the house seemed to still be sleeping, I went out walking in the city. I had visited it three or four times in the company of my father ten or fifteen years prior, crossing the great river over several hours of sailing from the Bajada Grande of the Paraná, beyond the troubled network of islands and creeks that separated the two main banks by several leagues. As my birthplace was a meager country house stacked atop the canyon that overlooked the river, the city always seemed enormous upon each visit: frenetic and brightly-colored, its inhabitants distinguished people well established in the world and engrossed in important business at all times. But now that I was returning after so many years, having detoured through Madrid, London, Paris, and even Buenos Aires, it was reduced to its actual proportions in my eyes, before which such true cities had passed; as is often the case for most people, the city that remained an unchanging image in my memory had shrunk in reality, as if external things existed in several dimensions at once. The city proper stretched out for a few blocks around the plaza in straight, sandy streets, largely unpaved, running parallel or perpendicular to the river, with a couple of churches; a council building, a long structure that was also the customs-house, jail, hospital, and police station; single-story houses with tiled roofs and barred windows so low they seemed to come out of the ground; and fruit trees, too: oranges, tangerines, and lemon trees laden with fruit, fig and peach trees bare in the cold, loquats, little fields of prickly pear, enormous acacias, jacarandas, medicinal *lapacho* trees, silk floss, and red-flowered *ceibos*, and weeping willows that abounded near the water. Orchards and farmyards opened onto back courtyards. In the outer districts, brick or tile-and-adobe houses were less common, and the hovels were spaced farther apart, were dirtier and more wretched, but downtown, a number of businesses had opened in the area immediately surrounding the plaza, and the streets bordering it had been paved. In the old church of Saint Francis, which the Indian converts had helped construct and decorate, was a convent and, five or six blocks from the council building, a house that sheltered several nuns. Of the five or six thousand city-dwellers, very few seemed to have left their houses that morning, perhaps on account of the cold, but I knew that all the city's riches—cattle, timber, cotton, tobacco, leathers—came from the countryside, and it was clear at that early hour that there was next to nothing to do in the frigid and deserted streets. All the shops were still closed around the plaza. I went walking by the riverside, and I saw a few men fishing on horseback: The two riders entered the water with a net suspended between them to dredge the bottom and then, with a vigorous folding motion, cast the net onto the bank where fish fell twitching on the sand. One of the fish managed such a violent and desperate contortion that, leaping up to a considerable height, it fell back into the water and did not show itself again, which seemed quite comical to the fishermen, who guffawed on and on in noisy celebration.

My stroll had been too early, for it was not yet eight-thirty when I returned to the Parra house, and the family had just awoken. We arranged ourselves, Señor Parra and I, in a large room next to the kitchen, which doubtless served as a dining room on ordinary days, and a negro youth prepared us *mate* and brought us warm cakes from the kitchen. The night before, we had eaten in a slightly more luxurious dining room, reserved for special occasions, but in the modest room where we took breakfast, proximity to the kitchen made the air warmer and more agreeable, as the adjoining stoves were nearly always lit in the wintertime. We had barely touched on the subject of his son, Prudencio, when Señor Parra openly and meekly offered himself up to my questions.

Young Prudencio Parra, just turned twenty-three, had fallen into a deep stupor for some months, a state that, in truth, was the culmination of a series of attacks, each one proving graver over time. Young Prudencio had acted strangely since puberty, but only in the last two or three years might his behavior be considered a state of derangement. What had been mere peculiarities at first were degenerating little by little into madness. At thirteen or fourteen, he spent whole days shut away in his bedroom filling notebook after notebook with "moral reflections" (as he called them) only to build an enormous bonfire in the basement of the house a few months later, using those and other papers blackened with his near-illegible handwriting, declaring that from that day forth he would wholeheartedly dedicate himself to good works; but those changes in humor, however, had not unsettled the family, as they attributed them to the sudden but short-lived excesses of passion that are unique to youth. The tendency toward shifting moods seemed, for its part, inherent to his temperament; since early childhood, these abrupt changes had been observed not only by the family, but also by the nurses—who, slaves or not, were practically part of the family—and nobody took it seriously, to the point that the young man's instabilities had become part of the household's tradition of comic anecdotes. But since eighteen or so, things had grown more serious, and the gravity of the situation was evident. His bouts of melancholy were becoming more frequent and more acute. Several doctors, from the city or passing through, had examined him and prescribed him treatment, with no visible result. Señor Parra was a sensible enough man not to believe the rumors of demonic possession or witchcraft that raced through the city, and, not exactly among the less affluent strata of the population, but he had scruple enough not to hide them and even conveyed all the details to me, allowing me to prove once more how the powers of science might save mankind—not just those living in faraway regions of the planet, but also in supposedly enlightened European empires—from the ignorance and pain, for superstition and obscurantism had added defamation and slander to the case of young Prudencio, as if his grievous illness was not enough. According to Señor Parra, Prudencio was seized by such a frenzy for philosophical study that he read day and night, and when he'd exhausted the local libraries, which were few and sparse, he would order books from Córdoba, Buenos Aires, or Europe, so desirous of receiving them that, while he waited, he would go to the port every day to ask at the arriving ships if they had his books. But after a time a sort of despondency overtook him, and what once had been sheer enthusiasm, energy, and jubilation, turned to reluctance, dejection, sighs. He began to grumble that nature had not granted him the faculties required to study science and philosophy, and that only a foolish and overweening pride had made him err, comparing himself to the great geniuses, humanity's benefactors like Plato and Aristotle, Aquinas and Voltaire. As I inferred from Señor Parra's tale, the subject of his ineptitude for study tormented Prudencio for many months, and bit by bit he attributed to this supposed ineptitude a series of irreparable wrongs he believed he had committed, such that after a time he began to think himself responsible for great troubles—or mere mishaps—in the city, as well as those he learned of from the gazettes arriving from Buenos Aires or the Court. When that undue sense of duty did not reduce him to a weeks-long prostration, during which he would not leave his room, or even his bed, for anything, it would cause him spells of fever, during which it seemed by all means necessary that he act immediately to prevent certain catastrophes, though it was always impossible to get a further explanation. Several times, according to Señor Parra, he'd searched for ragged and dirty garments, preferring those that had belonged to slaves but were in such a state that even the slaves no longer used them, and, bare-headed and barefoot, had taken to the streets to read on the corners some supposedly philosophical tract that he himself had incomprehensibly drawn up. According to Señor Parra, Prudencio's handwriting had changed completely and his minute and firmly-applied adolescent script—unreadable even then—had transformed into a monumental, disjointed one, so loose, overblown, and shaky that no more than twenty or thirty words fit into a notebook. People generally took pity on him and brought him back to the house, but once a few ill-favored sorts, vagrants who roamed the outskirts, had taken him to amuse themselves at his expense. They abandoned him afterward in the middle of a field where he had wandered all night; the search party just managed to find him the following day. Señor Parra told me that when they found him, Prudencio hadn't seemed at all upset by the humiliations visited upon him; rather, it was the vagabonds' lot that troubled him, and he was insistent, exciting himself almost to tears, about the poverty that had forced them to the margins of society. A week later, when the police captured two members of the band who had returned to the city thinking they would not be recognized by more than a few residents, they got a few good lashes and were tied to stakes in a little field near the edge of town, where Prudencio went to see them and begged the authorities to release them. With time, those fits would pass, and a sadness overtook him, heavier each time. (Señor Parra explained to me that during that period Prudencio's handwriting would change back, shrinking once more, but so exaggeratedly that it became illegible. What's more, from then on he left off writing altogether. So said Señor Parra.)

He did not wash or dress, and sometimes did not even get out of bed, and a sort of apathy took hold of him; despite his peculiarities, he'd been very affectionate since boyhood, not only with family members, but also with neighbors, the slaves, and even strangers, to the point that sometimes his demonstrations proved too much and annoyed certain people who were only passing through the house—but that affection had gone, as if the real world where he had lived until that time was being replaced by another where everything was gray and strange. Troubles, illnesses, and even the deaths of those who had previously been very dear to him yielded not a single sentiment or emotion, and if from time to time his breathing and occasional moans betrayed his undeniable suffering, it was impossible to know what caused it. It became clear, though, that the causes were not external, but lay rather in a few small, painful thoughts that seemed to be unchanging and constantly pondered. Señor Parra had to begin forcing Prudencio out of bed, to dress, to eat, to take a walk, or at least go out to the gallery or the courtyard, especially when the weather was fair, and though he protested at first, in the end, meekly, he would let himself be led away. His eloquence, which he employed during bouts of fever to try to convince his fellow men that a hazy but imminent catastrophe was brewing, began to wane, and his impassioned speeches became more incoherent and lacked conviction. Gestures and signs once accompanied them for emphasis and to suggest, especially, a secret that he tried in his passion to pass on to his fellows without revealing it completely, but little by little his rants broke down, and exclamations were replaced by halting and unfinished sentences, joining the stiffness of his expression and the feeble immobility of his limbs. In the end, he would only open his mouth to answer, and only in monosyllables, a question he had been asked. When from time to time he made an effort to give a slightly more detailed response, he would form two or three confused and faltering sentences, uttered weakly as if all energy had abandoned him. And in recent months, his prostration had been total, but a curious detail of his behavior, strange as it was to say the least, had come to light: He had closed his left hand in a fist and held it clenched tightly ever since. When asked the reason for his gesture, he would turn his head and press his lips together to make it clear that he was unwilling to answer, and the few times several family members tried to make him open his fist to see what would happen, at times even just for sport, he had resisted so frantically that his relatives had stopped out of pity and left him in peace. One day, Señor Parra noticed that Prudencio's hand was bleeding; it dawned on him that all that time, his son's fingernails had continued to grow, digging into the soft flesh of his palm, so he really did have to make him open the fist to cut his nails and care for his wounds. According to Señor Parra, young Prudencio had begun to howl and thrash about on the floor, trying to stop them from opening his fist, making such a racket that the neighbors came running, believing a crime had been committed in the house. Despite young Prudencio's extreme weakness from his prostration and loss of appetite, his resistance was so great that they needed three or four strong men to hold him down, open his fist, and keep the hand open while they clipped his nails and tended to his cuts, which had become infected. For the length of the operation, Prudencio howled or whimpered with such a look of terror that the men pitied him, but many of those present noticed Prudencio peering nervously up at the room's ceiling and walls as if he feared they would come down on him. The whole scene had reminded Señor Parra of a time when he (Señor Parra) was a boy, awoken from a hideous nightmare screaming and crying, and as the faces of his family inclined solicitously over him and tried to calm him with words, caresses, and meaningless gestures, he had sensed that, despite how close their bodies seemed, they were in two different worlds: they, in the unreal world of appearances and he, in the true, real one that he saw in his nightmare. According to Señor Parra, his son finally seemed to quiet somewhat, and though his sobs came further and further apart, the whimpering contin-ued, broken by an occasional breath. Lying on the bed, his father and two slaves pinning him firmly while the doctor tended to his wounds, Prudencio signaled for them to free his right hand. When he got what he wanted, he drew it near, a little shyly, to the injury in such a way that when he was almost close enough to obstruct the doctor's work, he motioned over the wounded hand with the healthy one as if snatching an insect from flight, and closed his right fist around it, which seemed to calm him completely. While the bandages on his left hand remained, according to Señor Parra, Prudencio kept the right fist closed, but when they were removed few days later, he changed back to the left hand. Since then, he agreed to open the fist every ten to fifteen days for his nails to be cut, but before he opened it, he would carry out the strange opera-tion with the other hand, snatching something from flight that he apparently would not allow to escape for anything in the world. Señor Parra explained to me that his son undertook this curious procedure with the absolute and utmost care, and that every time he watched him do so confirmed that it was carried out with the devotion of a ritual.

Before leading me to his son's room, Señor Parra, answering a query of mine, told me of the treatments prescribed by the previous doctors who had examined Prudencio, none of which yielded the slightest result. The two doctors, chapter-certified for ongoing practice in the city, had treated him in the typical fashion, but barely saw him on their visits now, declaring him incurable. Another two or three doctors who were passing through the city were consulted, and one of them had recommended baths in the Salado River, declaring the quality of its water and especially of its clay most advisable in the treatment of melancholia. Señor Parra told me that although Prudencio was terrified to plunge into the river, he readily consented to being thoroughly coated with the banks' reddish mud and would sprawl in the sun to dry, to the point that it was almost always a struggle to remove the layer of crusted clay that covered him. The previous summer, however, his stupor had become so serious that it had been impossible to take him from his room and bring him to the riverbank.

Señor Parra led me to his son's room. A smell of enclosure, of strange substances mixed and marinated—of abandonment—pervaded despite the order that reigned within the soberly furnished bedroom, overheated by the brazier installed by the window to be burnt all night. Young Prudencio was propped up in bed, under blankets, sunk into the shadows, and his head, topped with a white nightcap, lolled on a heap of pillows. Although its occupant's eyes were closed, the bed looked as though it had just been made, but Señor Parra explained to me that the young man remained completely immobile as he slept, so in the morning the bed always gave the impression of being untouched. Prudencio's face had a jaundiced appearance, especially striking beneath the sparse beard that covered his chin and jaw, and also because of his severely narrow features. A sort of vertical crease that ran from cheekbone almost to jaw cut his left cheek in two, while the right cheek sunk into an enormous cleft that took it up entirely, like the remains of a territory following a landslide. Despite his youth, his skin was wrinkled like worn leather, stretched across his cheekbones so the contours took on a cartilaginous sheen. But his forehead in particular drew the attention, crisscrossed with deep horizontal folds, and on his brow a horseshoe-shaped crease, as if a tiny brand had been embedded in his flesh, joined the two eyebrows with a deep furrow. Beneath the nightcap, tufts of hair bunched long and stiff against the pillow, further accentuating the thinness of his face. For some mysterious reason, the points of two white bits of cloth emerged from his ears, stuffed in the openings. Though his eyes were closed, the suffering was plain on his face, from the deep wrinkles of course, but also from his heavy eyelids and gaping mouth. It was a bottomless pain and, truthfully, rather a theatrical one, as though his expressions were exaggerated to make it plainer, with the effect of adding decades of dejection, adversity, and affliction to his mere twenty-three years. Despite his half-closed eyes, it was hard to know if he was sleeping or pretending to sleep, but he lay so still that it seemed genuine and, along with his yellowed pallor, gave him the look of a cadaver. But when I leaned down to draw back the blankets and examine the rest of his body, he slowly drew his eyelids up, in stages, one might say, and let his gaze slip indifferently over me, landing on some unknown spot between the bed and door. I was surprised to discover he was not as thin as I had expected, at least if the knee-length white nightgown did not mislead me, but his torso seemed fleshier than his face, and his calves—ending in enormous feet, gently resting one beside the other, with plump, widely-spaced toes—did not seem thin or fragile. His right arm, open-handed, lay along the length of his body, but the left fist, resting on his abdomen, was closed so tightly that the effort further whitened the yellowish skin of his protuberant knuckles. The general softness of his body; his ravaged face; the cottony neglect of his limbs; the passivity of his great, motionless feet; his lost gaze and suffering expression—it all contrasted with the determination of the closed fist where all the body's energies seemed to gather, and thus it was plain to see that this gesture, which, to many, represented nothing more than an irrational and chimeric stubbornness, was to me a matter of life or death that I, in that moment, would have been crazy to ignore. I know, too, that only insanity dares to render those limits of thought that good sense, for the sake of remaining sensible, often prefers to ignore— that it drives the mad to be detached, stubborn, beyond recovery. Something horrifyingly serious seemed to depend on that hand, and the painful determination of his gesture made me believe that in the event that his concentration waned and his tension slack-ened, letting the hand relax, weak once more, an apocalyptic wind would start to blow, dragging all the universe in its wake. I studied his body for a few seconds without perceiving the slightest move-ment; once open, his eyes did not close, once more demonstrating my teacher's frequent observation, namely that the mentally ill are able to do things with their bodies that are forbidden to the sane; to verify more thoroughly, I concentrated on detecting external signs of respiratory activity, such as the soft sound of exhalation and inhalation or thoracic expansion and contraction, but after several seconds I was forced to admit that utter silence reigned in the room and his body stayed perfectly motionless. Paradoxically, from that immobility emanated not a sense of death, but rather an impression of struggle, of adversarial forces in perpetual conflict that had chosen that boy's body and soul as their battlefield. His fixed and slitted eyes, his body's utter stillness, and the fist held tight against his abdomen gave the impression that all his interest concentrated on some remote, internal region where said decisive battle was taking place, to capture even the tiniest details of that faraway tumult.

When we left the bedroom, Señor Parra looked at me searchingly, trying to ascertain my opinion of his son's condition, and I responded in all sincerity: As experience had shown that fits of stupor never lasted overly long, and as at first glance young Prudencio's physical condition did not appear to have deteriorated, he might hope to improve somewhat in the coming months. (In fact, it happened that he recovered when we embarked on the journey to Casa de Salud; almost in the very moment we left the city, our patient came out of his stupor. Later on, I will record his strange evolution in detail.)

Señor Parra showed me his house, as he had not been able to the previous night owing to the lateness of my arrival, and I, out of discretion, had refrained from roaming that morning while the masters slept. The classical rows of rooms that opened out onto galleries, forming square courtyards—the slaves slept in the back rooms—held not a single surprise for me, but out behind them was a well-tended, if cold-ravaged, garden and a fine nursery of fruit trees, laden with mandarins, oranges, lemons. As we talked, we ate a few mandarins, sweet and icy cold, at the foot of the tree, and when we went back inside, I was surprised by something that the house's conventional construction had been unable to give me: I stepped into one of the rooms next to the dining room, tastefully furnished and endowed with an abundant library. Several local landscapes, executed by an able but uninspired hand, adorned the walls, and a bust of Voltaire observed us from a shelf. I suddenly realized that I was lucky to be staying at the house of a fashionable and illustrious family, a most rare situation in those remote provinces at that time. (*The situation has not, in fact, improved.* Note, M. Soldi.) Señor Parra's discretion, not to mention his shyness, prevented him from revealing too much (and perhaps also my reputation as Dr. Weiss's collaborator and having studied in Europe), but over the weeks I was forced to tarry, I was able to learn of his lively and sensible ideas and the agreeable tenor that prevailed within his family, who were truly saddened by young Prudencio's illness. The paintings in the library were by Señor Parra, which, when I found out, caused me to judge them more favorably—I do not know if this was because they had been executed by an amateur who had never undertaken to study painting, or out of affection for the artist and his family. Señor Parra's numerous businesses, which had allowed him to amass a considerable fortune, did not prevent him from cultivating himself as well as his orchard and garden, and his genuine modesty was unjustified if one takes into account the soundness of his general opinions—a rare trait in a man of means—as it had already been made possible for me to note more than once, by observing frequently on two continents, that the rich hold a high opinion of themselves and are, by a mysterious transposition, convinced that their skill at winning money allows them to hold forth topics of which they are ignorant, whether artistic, political, or philosophical.

While Señor Parra went to carry out his duties, I went to the barracks to see if my traveling companions had settled in. The soldiers, accustomed to military life, had already melted in with the rest of the troops—perhaps too lofty a name for that handful of men, poorly-armed and practically in rags—but Osuna was in a foul mood and claimed not to have slept all night from the racket and constant bustle that reigned in the block. What they called "the block" was an old brick-and-adobe building, in fairly poor repair but large enough to permit some forty men to spread out their nicked, scuffed equipment on the hard-packed floor and kip down at night. Special cases, like sick men or deserters, I would learn later, were dispatched to the hospital or the jail, which were located in a slightly larger building perhaps a hundred meters from the block. Osuna's discontent seemed justified because the accommodations were of the worst sort, but, visiting it some time later, I saw that our guide's rather special character might have caused him to exaggerate the reasons for his protest without realizing it. It ought to be clear to my future readers, should ever I have them, that this observation does not denigrate Osuna's many and excellent qualities in any way, as his loyalty, matchless efficiency, intelligence, common sense, and self-denial overshadowed those others. And yet, I do not know whether due to professional bias or something else, it is impossible for me not to speculate about personality traits that motivate the opinions and actions of those I consort with beyond the reasons they themselves might offer, which are likely true enough. Osuna was thirty-five at the time and already knew the vast plain minutely, out to its farthest corners, and he had turned his irrefutable knowledge of everything related to it into a profitable but unsteady situation, perhaps familiar to the sage or the artist. Like Osuna or other desert-experts of his kind, the wise man or the artist must frequently deal with those who may benefit from their practice but are unable to properly appreciate it. Leaving aside the fact that the others did not stop to consider the sacrifices made to acquire that knowledge—and in Osuna's case that knowledge constituted a true mastery of the unseen—it could leave him in fairly tight situations. These included dealing with superiors who might fail to give him the respect he deserved, merely taking advantage of his knowledge, or, might instead form an excessive regard for him, giving him special treatment that cut him off from the soldiers and men of similar means. Because of the many travails that gave rise to his knowledge, Osuna had acquired a particular character that made him feel darkly different from the rest, separating himself from them and concentrating, like a great ascetic, on the many details of the outer world. Over the years I dealt with him, I noticed that he was at ease only in the desert. What astonished me about him was seeing, when we made camp at some outpost and he was tempted by liquor, how the impassive façade began to crack on his sharp, dark face, how his small, slanting eyes sparkled, rapid and ever-changing, betraying the passions he hid so well during the day: vanity, arrogance even, regarding his position; jealousy that kept him from admitting to himself that there might be some other worthy guide on the plain; his efforts, otherwise so clumsy, to always be the center of attention; his air of superiority as he listened to and observed the other gauchos, soldiers, et cetera, who shared a bit of roast with the travelers in the plain's empty night. But much more astonishing to me was to see him decisively mount his horse the next morning, fresh and ready; laconic, energetic, forbidding his face from revealing a single emotion, a single sentiment—as opposed to some hours earlier—as if it was not his will to pick up the road again, proceeding thanks to the thousand messages only he could read that reality sent to him at every step. So every time Osuna complained of something to me and I proposed to rectify the situation, he would respond that it wasn't worth it. My hearing his complaints, it seemed, was enough.

The length of our stay in the city depended on two patients, one who hailed from Asunción in Paraguay and the other from Córdoba, joining the other two in the city, young Prudencio Parra and a nun who, as the Mother Superior informed us by letter, had fallen into madness after being violated in the convent garden. The man was in jail and the nun remained in the convent, but her constant agitation convinced the local religious authorities to appeal to Dr. Weiss to resolve the problem. In recent months, a copious exchange of letters had flown between Las Tres Acacias and the four patients' families to arrive at an agreement about the conditions of transport, admission, treatment, fees, et cetera, and those lengthy negotiations had prompted our arrival in the city where, once the four patients had been gathered along with the guards and all that was necessary for the voyage, the caravan would depart. At first we had planned to undertake the voyage by water, but the special cargo we had to transport dissuaded the few Italian sailors whose ships provided the accommodations necessary to do so. Besides, we were reluctant about transferring the mad on the waterways because, unless we kept them locked in the hold the entire time, the wild river might prove a danger to the patients. Finally, with the families' explicit consent, and as the result of negotiations carried out personally by Dr. Weiss, we adopted the solution of a land voyage, never thinking for an instant that, after weeks of swelling hour by hour, the river whose company we rejected would come for us, rising up of its own accord to impose its harsh rule.

For the patients' comfort, we had rented five covered wagons of the sort travelers use to pass over the dangerous roads of that vast territory, the trade routes from Buenos Aires to Chile, on the other side of the mountains. Those carriages were pulled not by a pair of oxen like cargo wagons but rather by horses, and even boasted a door and windows, fixed up inside like little enclosures that were at once bedroom and living room, of the most cramped and rudimentary sort, of course, but with the necessary comforts to endure the interminable desert crossing, and above all to allow for (more or less) reasonable sleep at every stop on the way. Four of the wagons were intended for the patients and the fifth went to me, although I would have made do with a tent to share in the luck of the troops who would accompany us. The wagons all belonged to the same owner, a tradesman from Buenos Aires who did business in the Tucumán province, Córdoba, and Mendoza; in various Chilean cities; and with everyone in the littoral, where he had to compete with river transport; to Asunción in Paraguay, where his family had originated. The rental conditions were quite favorable because one of the patients belonged to the owner's family. Part of the escort would leave from the city, Santa Fé, meeting us halfway down the road between Asunción and Buenos Aires, and as the road from Córdoba also passed close by, that city was the logical meeting point. We calculated that the trip to Casa de Salud would take some fifteen days, already trying not to force the march too much so as not to overtire our patients, but the various obstacles that arose and the grave circumstances that turned us from our course, that blocked our way and even forced a retreat, multiplied the duration nearly threefold.

That very afternoon I sent a message to the convent announcing my arrival for the following day. The Mother Superior, a severe-looking woman in her fifties, received me at eleven in the morning in a clean and frigid room, and from the first sentences we exchanged I realized that my profession caused her deep discomfort, but that the case of Sister Teresita, the nun Dr. Weiss was to look after, appeared even worse than before, and would doubtless bring them no few problems, as they would not otherwise deign to resort to us. In the course of the conversation, however, I learned that the order to engage Dr. Weiss's services had come from Buenos Aires. During my interview with the Mother Superior, I was unable to stop smiling to myself, in the face of further proof that madness, simply by its presence, disrupts and even destroys the endeavors, hierarchies, and principles of the people we deem sane. The Mother wanted to extract an absurd, explicit promise of discretion on my part, and to her barely pertinent and almost offensive insistence, I said coldly that an explicit promise in that particular case would be superfluous, as discretion, since Hippocrates, had been the founding principle of our science. Without reacting to the firmness of my response, but lowering her eyes so our gazes did not meet for the length of her tale, the Mother Superior told me, with many insinuations and roundabout phrases,

66

struggling mightily with her understandable modesty about the terrible nature of the facts she was relating, the story of Sister Teresita. The nun, who had first come to Peru from Spain, and who by the will of her order, the Handmaids of the Blessed Sacrament, had been transferred to the city, was, according to the Mother Superior, a rather naïve person and terribly devoted, given even to certain mystical excesses that had earned her several reprimands and calls to order. Despite her humble birth and lack of education beyond the essentials required for her religious training, she had a strong literary inclination that she used to express, according to the Mother Superior, her devotion to Christ and the Blessed Sacrament. One of the order's principle tasks was to look after women of ill repute who, unfortunately, according to the Mother Superior (*and,* I thought to myself, *to the approval of my teacher*) abounded in America. It was a ministry the young sister had dedicated herself to with unbridled passion, just as with all she undertook, visiting them too frequently and familiarly, which gave rise to certain misunderstandings. The young sister's intensity, which always manifested itself far too spontaneously, had fueled town gossip, as the inhabitants' perpetual idleness, according to the Mother Superior, engendered a fatal tendency to meddle in the lives of others. But according to the Mother Superior, that was no great thing relative to the real drama that had taken place at the end of last year. A man they had hired to tend the garden, orchard, and farmyard—according to the Mother Superior, there were so many unemployed in the city that it was safer to hire them for something, for otherwise they'd turn into vagabonds and criminals—who had been working for the convent for several months, began to abuse the young sister in secret, submitting her to every type of bestial humiliation, and threatened to kill her if she dared tell anyone. Naturally, the Mother Superior omitted the details that were too painful, but it did not take much to understand, from the red spots burning on her cheeks, that the memory of those details provoked strong emotions. One day, during the siesta hour, she, the Mother Superior, had come upon them in the little chapel, sprawled at the foot of the altar, engaging in, according to her, the sacrilege of animalistic satisfaction of carnal instincts. The gardener had been arrested straightaway and remained in jail, but the consequences had been devastating for Sister Teresita, to the point that she had lost her mind. The young sister was fragile by nature, and in the months leading up to what happened, she, the Mother Superior, had observed the signs of a stronger disturbance than usual in Sister Teresita, never imagining at any point, however, that those minor agitations, that attenuated but constant instability, the sudden shift from laughter to tears, and her excessive devotion to the Cruci-fied One, once exacerbated by the sordid drama that would touch her life, would precipitate into madness. While lulls passed in the midst of her unrest, and one might not detect the presence of mad-ness by looking at her, the Mother Superior went on to explain that her rapid changes in behavior were so very unexpected, the altered manners and language, that at first several members of the Church had believed themselves to be facing a case of demonic possession. They debated the possibility of sending her to the Inquisition, but the city's priest and exorcist, taking into account the fact the young sister had been the victim of such humiliations, believed there was an exact, known cause for her actions and that matters ought to be placed in the hands of justice and medicine. The ecclesiastical authorities in Buenos Aires had ruled on the case in the same way. Among those the Mother Superior cited, I recognized two who, contrary to the fairly widespread opinion of influential clergy-men, were favorably inclined to Dr. Weiss's therapeutic methods. As I saw it, choosing the case's gnoseological interpretation at the expense of the demonological interpretation was less a question of common sense on the part of the ecclesiastical authorities than

68

a wish for discretion. I had spoken many times with Dr. Weiss about an undeniable fact, namely that, for the past two centuries in Europe, the dungeons of most mental hospitals had been discreetly filled with wretches unfortunate enough to have been too sensational to commit to the bonfires. But the prison's tragic role, an embarrassing one many families believed we sought to perform, protected our specialty's emergence in the Parisian hospitals and its necessary evolution, which was the constant reflection in the Casa under the enlightened direction of my teacher. For us, the rigorous practice of medical science was the only possible form of charity.

The lengthy conversation was not without discomfort on both of our parts, as evidenced by our mutual reticence, and afterward I knew I could not gain an accurate idea of Sister Teresita's condition if I did not take the opportunity to see her myself; I explained to the Mother Superior that my professional obligation required me to see the patient immediately, and despite her visible hesitation, she ultimately agreed. The patient was in a room in the basement of the house under lock and key. The first thing I noticed in that narrow room was that the grille-covered window looked onto the gallery and courtyard, not the street. As the shutters were closed, the room was all in shadow at that moment, and we arrived dazzled by the clear, midday winter light, so for a few seconds I could not see much except a lively gray blot that emerged from a corner and came toward us, stopping in the center of the room. I stood blinking at the threshold, but the Mother Superior entered and went over to the window, prudently opening the shutters halfway. A ray of sun came in and lit up the girl with the intensity of a spotlight. She was rather petite and had very short hair, and, instead of the order's habit, she wore a sort of gray blouse that covered her from the neck, where it buttoned tightly, to her ankles. Although the room was freezing, I saw that her feet were bare on the brick floor, but she seemed unbothered by the cold. Noting the disapproval in my gaze, the Mother Superior rushed to explain that the sister wouldn't tolerate a brazier, as she had violent hot spells and declared that the cold had no effect on her. I searched for Sister Teresita's gaze to confirm what I had just heard, but I found it impossible to meet; she had gone still, eyes closed and a shy smile on her lips, the hands that emerged from the gray shirt-cuffs of her blouse resting softly on her belly, one atop the other. That overly-obvious shyness was not unfamiliar to me: It was not difficult to identify an attitude of fakery, common in certain mental patients brought before a doctor for the first time, of adopting a theatrical pose to try to persuade him, that it would be an unjustified waste of time to bother with people so normal to the naked eye as they. In presenting herself so calmly and demurely, there was also an attempt at seduction, quite effective on her part and ultimately unnecessary, as I must confess that her lively and energetic presence captured my sympathies immediately, though I did not let myself forget the strong likelihood that I was addressing a sick person. It did not take me long to realize Sister Teresita was trying to establish some private bond with me, not just apart from the Mother Superior but perhaps also apart from the convent and even the world, maybe to prove to them, and also to herself, that she and her actions could once and for all be properly interpreted.

When I approached her, she opened her eyes and looked at me: She had round, gray little eyes, too restless there between her broad, domed forehead and her small nose, a round, pale little button with almost no septum, a single fleshy bump protruding above her thin lips, which remained closed all the while. Her tiny white face, a circle drawn from where her hair emerged above her bulging forehead, outlined her pink-dusted cheeks and closed at her delicate, almost nonexistent, chin. It was hard not to love her at once, with the same love one has for a pet rabbit, for example, knowing that its hot and nervous existence will bring us more complications than happiness once we adopt them—their motives, so different from our own, count ours for nothing. When our gazes met, I thought I perceived fleeting sparks of mockery in hers, that sort of tacit mockery with which, in the presence of third parties, certain people acknowledge us, believing we share the same point of view about things; in reality, it is a search for complicity, and usually a fruitless one. The Mother Superior noticed it right away and, more worried about morality than the health of her ward, went to Sister Teresita and encircled her shoulders with an arm concealed by the wide, black sleeve of her habit, exposing no more to the world of sin and corruption than a white, slightly wrinkled hand that alighted firmly but without violence on Sister Teresita's left shoulder. A detail that almost immediately attracted my attention, although frequent dealings with madness had accustomed me to that kind of dissonance, was the contrast I observed in the little nun, between the terrible humiliations she had borne for months, and the good humor, the air of health and determined energy reflected in her person. When I began to interview her, as pleasantly as possible, she adopted an attitude both childish and demure, curling up against the Mother Superior's chest so, I realized, the Mother Superior had to respond to my questions for the patient, who darted occasional glances at me from the corners of her eyes, provocative yet mocking. As the Mother Superior's answers added nothing new to what she had told me upon my reception, I chose to defer the interview for the coming days and took a moment to cast a glance about the room, ascertaining that the meticulous reigned therein: The bed was made without a wrinkle, with a sort of black cape spread carefully at the foot, and there was a table with a three-branched candelabra from whose stand not a single drop of wax had fallen, as well as two stacked books of equal size, a metalwork inkwell with two or three pens resting in the horizontal groove at

71

the base, a small rectangular pile of white, well-aligned papers, each one in its place, and a crude wooden chair whose rattan seat was tucked in beneath the table. Even the wicker cushion of the armchair from which she had arisen to see us enter seemed not to have a crease, not a dent, as if the small girl's body resting on it a few moments ago had been weightless and without substance.

When I expressed my wish to retire, announcing I would return a few days later to finish the preparations for departure, the Mother Superior, relieved perhaps, removed her arm from Sister Teresita's shoulders and approached me, intending to bring me to the front door. The little nun did not move from her spot but, abandoning the vulnerable attitude she had held a moment ago, she straightened up so the sunshine streaming through the window suddenly made her look bigger and stronger. A noise I could not at first identify began to carry through the room, until I realized that the little nun had grit her teeth and puffed her cheeks out slightly, building up saliva inside her mouth and making a screeching sound, and I was still wondering why when she began to writhe her tongue obscenely, moving it all about, licking her lips, thrusting it in and out of her mouth, rhythmic and rigid, and how, even as she carried out these movements, she was gathering spittle, drooling and screeching. A heightened expression of ecstasy came over her face and her eyelids drooped once more. She pushed her belly in and out while she slowly shook her head in rapture as, at the sides of her body, her hands made strange, slow movements. All this sudden activity, excepting perhaps the writhing of her tongue, reminded me of certain group dances I had seen the African slaves perform sometimes in the port of Buenos Aires, and it took me a few moments to realize that my astonishment at the little nun's contortions, presented somehow like a dance, came from the fact that they were carried out (apart from the saliva-choked screeching) in utter silence. The pink in her cheeks burned even brighter and, because of the effort it cost her to produce saliva, spread across her whole face, but when I turned to the Mother Superior, who had lost all reserve in my presence and looked at me, her expression helpless and supplicating, it was plain to see that redness—in her case of shame and confusion—had won out on her face, as well. Sister Teresita's outburst came to be of great use to me, however, as it allowed me to show great calm before the Mother Superior, which I did not refrain from exaggerating, to suggest to her how ordinary the little nun's behavior appeared in the eyes of science. When I saw that despite her so-called ecstasy, the little nun would sneak glances from time to time to see the effect her behavior had on us, I burst out laughing, which alarmed the Mother Superior but not so the little nun, who abandoned her strange posture and, having cheerfully contemplated us for a few satisfied moments, came toward us. Thirty years have passed since that morning, but I can still see clearly the curious way she moved then, throwing her torso forward and her buttocks slightly back, arms folded with elbows out and hands crossing each other rhythmically at her navel, a slight swing in her hips, adopting with her expression and agility, despite the apparent delicacy of her form, the masculine air of a young boy. Impudently, she planted herself a meter distant and wagged her left index finger, crooking it in to signal me to come closer; trying, amiable and firm, in the patient tone one might use with a disobedient child, she said: *Come here, and I'll suck it.* With a cry both overwhelmed and appalled, the Mother Superior hurled herself from the room, although she must have witnessed similar scenes many times. But among the mad I had seen far worse, and I have to say, there had been something amusing in the contrast between the little nun's crudeness and the excessive modesty of the Mother Superior, who was unable to see things from a medical angle, and so—without becoming the slightest bit upset, and trying not to appear shocked by anything—I approached the little nun with my best smile, explaining that I had not come for that, but rather to look after her as a doctor, and that as we were going to be living together from now on it was best that we maintained a good relationship. She burst out laughing and stuck out her tongue again, and tapped at it lightly with her finger, taking it into her mouth and asking: *So not like this . . . ?* I promised I would come by to see her that week and left the room. While the Mother Superior was locking up, Sister Teresita stood in the window behind the grille, and, in a cheery and playful tone, as if telling a secret the three of us would share, began to softly recite a list of horrifying obscenities, describing voluptuous acts that the Mother Superior and I were supposedly about to commit and from which she was unfairly excluded.

When we arrived at her chamber, I saw that the Mother Superior's eyes were full of tears and, taking pity, I tried to console her, explaining that madness ought not be judged by moral standards nor addressed within our usual categories of thought. After a time, the Mother Superior seemed to quiet and, as I bid her goodbye, I noticed her attitude toward me had changed; she appeared to have set aside her mistrust. However, when we parted, the unpleasant sensation remained that the Mother Superior had not told me the whole truth about the little nun.

A surprise witness would confirm this for me a few days later. Notified of my presence in the city, Dr. López, a local physician and friend to the Parra family, invited me to visit him—out of politeness to be sure, but also to discuss several matters important to the due practice of our profession, and to consult upon a few difficult cases he had been treating in the hospital. That hospital was once Jesuit and has since been restored to them on their return to America; if my information is correct, it was in those years under the charge of the Franciscans, who had, to put it one way, "annexed" the neighboring monastery. If anything can

74

suggest the general poverty that reigned in that city, and how only a few families were spared, it is the fact that the chapter-house, the hospital, and the jail operated out of the same building, a long *chorizo*, as the cheeky local idiom had come to name all constructions with a plan that, vertical or parallel to the street, extended in a single long line of rooms, or in two, separating at a courtyard and meeting at the front to form the building's main body. In this building, shaped then like a squared-off *U*, the façade, where the government, the administration, and a small police station were located, occupied an entire block on the main plaza, and of the two wings extending from the façade to the river, one lodged the hospital and the other, like its grimmer reflection across the courtyard, the jail and the customs-house.

Out of some fifteen patients, two or three thorny cases required a consultation—the rest posed no problem since a mere glance told me there would be no cure—and once we finished examining them, my colleague, an older man who impressed me with his clear experience and insight, glanced all around as if in fear of committing an indiscretion. He told me there was another case he wanted to submit to me, but that we would examine him in a chamber adjoining the common area, where he had his office. That said, he signaled to a male nurse who had been circling us persistently during our visit to the common area. The nurse left the office immediately and, through a window, I saw him briskly cross the courtyard toward the jail. As soon as we were settled in his office, my colleague explained the reason for all this intrigue: As everyone already knew that I had come to the city to fetch Sister Teresita for admission at Las Tres Acacias, the nurse, who was a cousin of the nun's supposed rapist, had begged the doctor to hear the convent gardener's version of events, which was quite different from the one issued by the ecclesiastical authorities. Only the fact of this contradiction had staved off the firing squad, but the gardener's defenders had not managed to dispel the threat altogether. Dr. López was convinced that the gardener spoke the truth, and he had the utmost confidence in the cousin, his main collaborator for years. A small clerical faction supported him, especially among the Franciscans, but the Church refused to admit that the little nun's conduct—the hypothesis of a demonic intervention had been rejected—was due to, as it were, *natural* if inexplicable causes, and preferred, perhaps in the hope that the sin of some person outside the Church might explain the events, to maintain the gardener's guilt. The doctor told me the gardener admitted to having had carnal relations with the little nun, but he denied in the most energetic, even horrified, fashion, having violated her and particularly insisted that, if they had been found in circumstances that might be considered sacrilegious, it had been unexpected and against his will.

A few minutes later I heard, in greater detail, that version of events from the gardener's very mouth. Despite suffering months in prison, his appearance was that of a vigorous man and his manners those of an honorable person, and he must have been younger than his air—that of being overwhelmed by the situation—made him appear. His story seemed all too plausible, especially his description of the little nun's behavior, so well did it coincide with several similar cases I had treated with Dr. Weiss, and the gardener could not have invented certain characteristic details of that type of derangement on his own. In the transcript I made of his words I will address the obligation, as I believe I have already warned above, of using several terms and turns of phrase that might sound overly harsh to certain listeners who—with all due respect—consider themselves decent, but it is necessary to keep in mind that, in mental illness, the afflicted subjects' vocabulary and conduct differ completely from those of healthy persons. (The use of Latin borrowed for the scientific tract seems out of place in the case of this personal report, which addresses hypothetical readers. I cannot prejudge if they will or will not be men of science, a detail, for its part, that is secondary to the present manuscript. But as a more general reflection: What can be the aim of putting certain parts of the body and certain acts into Latin that, without Latin or any language at all, humans and animals use and carry out every day?)

The gardener, from the very start of his story, proved his sincerity in several ways, acknowledging his carnal relations with Sister Teresita for example, and also always referring to the nun without the slightest animosity, as if despite all that happened and the precarious situation he found himself in, he had preserved the liveliest sympathies toward her. For the gardener, it was the Mother Superior who was refusing to see the facts as they had truly occurred. And another important detail that seemed to confirm the gardener's sincerity was the justification he gave for his conduct: According to him, it took a long time to realize the little nun was acting strangely, and that things she said or did, if he had attributed them at first to an unbridled lewdness, must have actually been caused by madness. The gardener stated that all the while it was he who had felt himself under the little nun's influence and that sometimes he even had the feeling she was subjecting him to a sort of violence. That inability to recognize madness is in no way unusual, and I would even dare assert that he is nothing out of the ordinary, that such inability was no phenomenon of isolated individuals, but rather of entire nations which, as history has already repeatedly shown, may be under an influence like the gardener, and driven into the abyss by the seemingly flawless logic of delusion, when in fact all logic has been abandoned.

The gardener said he had been working in the convent for a few months without even noticing the little nun, who, aside from youth, lacked any special charm, and that things would have doubtless continued that way if her insistent glances, which became most suggestive when they were alone—the gardener told us this in slightly coarser language than I now employ in writing thirty years later—hadn't attracted his attention, first intriguing him without a thought for what would happen later, but then drawing him in that direction. When he confided this to his cousin, who worked in the hospital, a fact that the cousin confirmed immediately, the cousin told him the little he knew of Sister Teresita: namely that, among their principal tasks, the Handmaids of the Blessed Sacrament cared for women of ill repute, and a few gossiped in the city—where young girls, as in every city, *think* they know everything even when they do not—that the young nun, who was overly familiar with women of ill repute and was sometimes peculiar in word and bearing, had a tendency to overstep the bounds of her mission. But everyone acknowledged her to be genuinely kind, and she was quite popular among the poor, especially those who had given themselves over to fallen ways—not just camp-following prostitutes or the harlots who plied their trade in shacks along the outskirts, but also deserters, cattle thieves, robbers, vagabonds, murderers. Some said they had seen her sitting in a hovel doorway, smoking a cigar, talking and laughing with a couple of whores. Others said she didn't decline to take a pull if someone thought to offer, and two or three even claimed to have seen her once, habit-sleeves rolled up, playing jackstones with a cluster of gauchos and soldiers on the porch of a general store. But they were only rumors. Of all those who circulated the stories, not a single one had, if pressed, been able to provide a witness for what was said. The gardener said the little nun was simply kind to him at first, but that one day, when he had gone into the chapel on a whim, he'd seen her climb the altar and rub the crucified Christ's drapery across his groin. On taking in the scene in the dim chapel, which he'd entered while still a little dazed from the brightness outside, he thought the little nun had been cleaning the statue, but he then saw her rise up on tiptoe from the chair she'd clambered up on to better reach the desired height, and the little nun began to lick the drapery in the same spot she had just been rubbing. The gardener had made a small, inadvertent noise that made her turn, peering into the half-light until she found him at the end of the chapel. The gardener said he was afraid that the little nun was going to dress him down on being caught, or become angry at the intruder who'd spied on her, but that, to his surprise, she didn't show the slightest alarm and smiled at him, and perched on the chair as she was, signaled to him to come closer. When the gardener told me this, it reminded me of the little nun's crooked index finger and innuendo-filled smile some days earlier, urging me to take a few steps toward her.

With the abrupt and evidence-filled sincerity of one who plays his final card to champion himself, the gardener told us, with the support of continued approving nods from his cousin and Dr. López, of his relations with Sister Teresita, which commenced within five minutes of their first meeting, on the little chapel's very floor, at the foot of the altar. According to the gardener, he'd resisted at first, precisely because of where they found themselves, but the little nun had convinced him, saying that nowhere in the Gospels or Church doctrines was the act they were about to per-form—or, in particular, the fact of carrying it out where they were preparing to do so—condemned by any text. She might be certain of this, though it is necessary to add that, due to the enormity of such acts, even the most punctilious Fathers of the Church, whom few possible circumstances of sin eluded, would have deemed it superfluous to condemn these acts explicitly. Further: According to the little nun, Christ had ordered her many times to consummate both carnal union with the human creature and divine union with the Holy Spirit. This would allow her to attain perfect union with

God, for Christ's divinity and his human nature had been separated anew upon his ascent to the Kingdom of Heaven, his divinity seated at the right hand of God and his humanity dispersed among men.

It is obvious that the gardener had been unable to express the above in such terms, so I should clarify that, to compile these details, I base them upon Sister Teresita's own writings: a roll of papers bundled together with blue ribbon that the nun secretly entrusted to the gardener when the scandal broke, and which the unlettered gardener left to his cousin the nurse, who brought it, finally, to Dr. López's study. The little nun's manuscript, titled *Manual for Love*, detailed a period of mystical delirium a few months before the episodes related by the gardener, and is a mix of prose and poetry in which Sister Teresita describes the passion she and Jesus Christ had shared ever since he first appeared to her in Upper Peru. It is worth noting that mental patients, when educated, can never resist the chance to express themselves in writing, trying to make their ramblings conform to the shape of a philosophical treatise or literary composition. It would be wrong to take them lightly, for those writings can be an invaluable source of significant data for a man of science; in the written word, he has at his disposal, safe from the transience of spoken ravings and fleeting actions, a series of thoughts preserved like insects fixed on a pin or a dried flower in an herbarium to be pored over by the naturalist. Hence, it seemed quite natural for my colleague to permanently entrust Sister Teresita's writings to me. (The matter of mysticism, even if we start from the hypothesis of its causal object's nonexistence, still warrants study, for if indeed the object is imaginary, the state that arouses belief in its reality is indisputably authentic. As in the fear of ghosts, for example, ghosts are of course nonexistent, but the fear is quite real, and as such merits thorough study, just like optics or the positions of the stars.)

In brief, the doctrine of the *Manual for Love* is a kind of dualism based upon the separation of the divine and the human in the wake of Christ's resurrection, and on the belief that love, whose essence is comprised of both elements, is the only force that can bring them together and realize their unity anew. Sister Teresita claimed that her doctrine had been revealed by Christ himself in Upper Peru, and as her attempts at carnal union with the Crucified One were impossible due to the metaphysical separation of the two worlds, she could only attain that unity by practicing physical love with the largest number of human beings possible, as such acts also involve the human and the divine. During the act, every human being who partook of spiritual and physical love became a reincarnation of Christ. To tell the truth, the *Manual*'s entire first part differs little or not at all from most Christian mystical writings—I might even say that Sister Teresita imitates them excessively, which explains certain archaisms in her style—but as one reads on, there is the painful sense that the author leaves off explaining the similarities of spiritual love and carnal love for the sole end of delighting in the description of physical love in all its variants, and toward the end, in the final pages (the text is unfinished), each idea becomes more incoherent than the last, the descriptions more lewd, and the prayers become mere lists of repeated obscenities. It was certainly not Sister Teresita's theological speculations, as the official superstition put forth far more ridiculous notions daily, that placed her in the hands of Dr. Weiss, but rather the affectedly salacious final portion and the frenzied enactment of her theology. A few months after being admitted to Casa de Salud, a curious development was engendered in Sister Teresita; her behavior reversed, becoming the opposite of what had led to her admission: Her passion for Christ was transformed bit by bit into a boundless hatred, and she could not look at a crucifix or icon without falling into a fit of rage, hurling insults and trampling them to pieces. At the same time, her wild penchant for obscenity, fornication, et cetera, grew into a violent aversion, and the youthful energy that so caught my attention when I first saw her turned to a kind of bovine passivity, enhanced by the fact that she was seized by an unwholesome voraciousness. After three years, the Church, which regularly sent visitors to the Casa to track the progress of her illness, decided she was cured, and the creature they sent back to Spain was a sort of meatball in a black habit, a silent woman of uncertain age who moved with the inertia and clumsiness of a cow, eyes dull and remote; the only outer sign of life was her red cheeks, smooth and shiny on her round face, swollen (it seemed) to the point of bursting.

But the order of my story is being corrupted. The gardener's case clearly proves a fact observed many times: Nothing is more contagious than delirium. From the story of that simple man, more confused than frightened by the situation in which he found himself, it took little effort to infer that, if he had let himself slide down that slope of lust and sacrilege with incomprehensible resignation, it was less because of her voluptuous ways than his credulity. Augustín—that was the gardener's name—was dazed by the theological arguments, mystical enthusiasm, and—as I have had means to prove so many times—the communicative sympathy of Sister Teresita, and had sincerely believed in the religious necessity of his acts and had lent himself for months to all the little nun's voluptuous caprices. Bearing in mind the first act they had performed at the foot of the altar and that, according to the gardener, the little nun was in the habit of talking to Christ over his shoulder during the act, it is not hard to imagine that what followed from that first sacrilege could not have been much wilder or more absurd. Curious as it seems, even while Augustín was enumerating those ludicrous aberrations that were to bring him before the firing squad, he appeared to continue to believe in the religious

82

meaning of their acts, and seemed to doubt neither the sincerity nor the necessity that caused Sister Teresita to drive him to his execution. She also seemed to harbor a particular fondness for the gardener until she left Casa de Salud and returned to Spain, and when she referred to him it was always warmly. During the journey to Casa de Salud, the little nun told me one day, lowering her voice and adopting a confidential tone, that they had Augustín locked in jail and wanted to shoot him *because he had such a big* . . . and accompanied her declaration with an obscene gesture, placing the palms of her hands some thirty centimeters apart and bobbing them up and down together suggestively. It was clear that, following this months-long intimate relationship, each one had been convinced of the other's innocence, and they were trying to convince everyone of this. The gardener, with a circumstantial line of argument, pleaded for himself and for Sister Teresita, and though the nun seemed to be unshakably certain regarding the source of her mission's legitimacy, which exempted her from apology or explanation for her conduct, she adopted an attitude of total indifference, even a cheerful lewdness, before her accusers. In every word and gesture, she showed her clear confidence in Augustín, whom she always spoke of not as a lover but as a friend, which perhaps exposed the gardener to even greater animosity from his accusers, though it cast a new light on the relationship to impartial observers. After practicing for so long in a number of European hospitals, I have had contact with nuns and other members of the clergy rather frequently, and though I have often met selfless, intelligent, obliging persons of good faith among them, I must record here that if you had to name a common feature in all of them, that feature would be the evident lack of any religious element in their thoughts and actions, which—that said—happened to greatly ease our relationship. Such people—compassionate, useful, and sensible—thanks to their naturally resistant constitutions, were impervious to all that is corrosive and devastating in religious feelings and ideas. Rather than mourn, we ought to be grateful that the religious temperament is such a rare phenomenon. Just as the world is full of good and bad poets, of thinkers both obvious and relevant, of ineffectual scientists, of false prophets and alleged men of God, so too have the truly religious been known to be greedy misers. I must state that, to my mind, the only truly religious person I have known in my life was Sister Teresita, and only briefly, for when she left Casa de Salud, lifeless and rotund, her little red button nose lost between ruddy cheeks, she was religious no longer. The love she felt for Christ had been intense and sincere, and it is pointless for me to speculate whether it manifested in a suitable form because, if that object of highest adoration truly exists, even if I were randomly set upon his appointed throne, it would be difficult to say which among all the different ways that his faithful have imagined to adore him is the proper one.

In Dr. López's study, the gardener's story announced, in closing, the catastrophe that soon followed: One day they were surprised in the sacrilegious act on the chapel floor before the altar, and the affair, once the Holy Office tribunal took up the matter, ended in the same place it had begun. After much deliberation and against Sister Teresita's obstinate contention that all acts committed had been ordained by Christ himself in Upper Peru in order to reestablish the unity of divine and human love that had been separated after the resurrection, the religious authorities ruled that Sister Teresita had lost her mind as the result of the violations and other repeated indignities the gardener had submitted her to; they put him in jail, where for several months he had been awaiting the trial that would surely condemn him to death. (Some time later, a letter from Dr. López informed me that, a few days before judgment took place, the gardener had managed to escape from prison, and, like so many others who, rightly or not, had accounts to settle with

Justice, disappeared into the plains. I received the news with relief and rushed to convey it to the little nun who, as her only comment, poked the tiny index finger of her right hand repeatedly into my stomach, a form of congratulation or recognition, as if Augustín's escape had been my work, and she approved with several slow nods.)

A private project during that professional trip had been, if my business allowed, to cross the Bajada Grande one day to visit the places where I had spent my childhood. As memories of my early years were no longer fresh, no emotional tie connected me to the far bank, for my family had returned to Spain upon my father's retirement from trade the year before Las Tres Acacias was founded. Yet it warmed my passions to anticipate the idea of crossing the great river and descrying the cliffs falling sheer into the red-hued water, as I had done so many times with my father when we returned from sailing among the islands. Unfortunately, the very cause of my prolonged delay in the city expanded ad nauseam the labor required to set out on my excursion, spoiling my plan: That year, the usual winter rise in those southern-flowing rivers, normally substantial, was treacherous, barbaric, and enormous. Treacherous because from hour to hour, minute to minute, and for months, water levels rose continually, submerging the coastal lands imperceptibly, bit by bit, farther from the banks each time; barbaric because, despite their surreptitious growth, a sudden swell overflowing the limits of the floodplains would cover a vast territory all at once, destroying everything in its path, and disrupting the life native to what would have been dry land and displace it from the banks, upsetting the customs, the roots, and very livelihood of men, animals, and plants, torn violently up from their usual spot and scattered until they were deposited, with savage anachronism, in the most unexpected corners of the region; and enormous because, due to that long and steady rise, the water, clouded with the new soil that fed into its path and taking on an uncertain hue that varied by location, perhaps sulfurous yellow, reddish-brown, or blackened and struck through with green filaments, won the westerly lands to the point of engulfing the plain, however far as an observer might travel on foot or by horse, across the entire visible horizon.

The flood at once detained the patients we awaited from Córdoba and Paraguay and confined us to the city. Everything was disrupted: the roads, the postal coach, the transport of goods. Departure and arrival times, already uncertain, became fickle and arbitrary, if not outrageous. Certain items not produced in the immediate surroundings, such as sugar, tea, and wine, began to run short. The prescient Señor Parra had gathered a little of everything in a room that served as larder and storehouse, whose key was in the hands of a slave charged with all matters related to questions of food and cooking. Señor Parra explained that in having so many people depend on him—relatives, employees, and slaves—it was his duty to anticipate possible events well in advance and down to the most trifling details, and to avoid setbacks as they arose. In those years, the isolated villages, many leagues distant from one another, scattered across that wild and endless desert, exposed their inhabitants to an array of dangers at every turn, requiring them to be ever vigilant. (Today, friends have informed me that threats come not from the desert, and that terror is unleashed not by the unchained elements, but rather by the government.)

Beyond the simplest daily tasks and regular visits to my two patients, I was left with no other occupation in that enforced idleness but observation, reflection, and reading. That I might partake of this last activity, Señor Parra placed his library at my disposal, a library which, as I believe I have mentioned, was most varied and abundant despite the city's isolation, and, as if this were not enough, and confirming the refinement of his character, he gifted me with six volumes of a French translation of Virgil, a poet for whom we discovered a mutual admiration, so that my reading of it, when time permitted, lasted until we finally sighted the snub, white building at Las Tres Acacias. For me, every challenge on our road is tied to a verse of Virgil, and to this very day the harsh sensations of travel and the subtle music of the verses bleed together in my memory, in a unique mingling that is mine alone, which will vanish from the world when I do. More than once I saw myself traveling the plain like Aeneas did the strange and hostile sea, and a deep emotion would overcome me when I glimpsed a fate for myself in the desert like that of Palinurus the helmsman who, startled from sleep, falls into the ocean, and his *naked corpse is doom'd on shores unknown to lie.* More than once I saw, more vividly than the dense and weighty things that surrounded me, the untimely pile of my bones gleaming white in the sun in some remote corner of the plain. But it is the fourth Bucolic that, among his short poems, remains my favorite to this day: the declaration of a golden age when so many catastrophes fly in the face of its unlikely coming, dependent not on the hero's armed will, but on a child's smile to the mother who bore him in her womb for nine heavy months; for that cheerful recognition of life, the poet promises the table of Jupiter and company of the goddess. And it is not irrational hope that gives rise to the vision: The new golden age will not be a prize or a conquest, but an undeserved gift from destiny and will come, not because men have won it, but because the Fates, someday, sometime, purely on a whim, will decree it.

He who has not seen, as I have, one of those lost cities of the plains on a rainy winter twilight when their first flickering lights begin to burn, with every visible object buried evenly beneath the double cloak of night and inclement weather—he does not know sorrow, though he might believe he has experienced it before. We were trapped by the flood, and the world's prison doubled, reinforced by that steely ring of water. But for the Parra family's affection, for the impassioned conversations with Dr. López and, above all, with Señor Parra, not one true sympathy tied me to anyone apart from the banal phrases and banal greetings exchanged as I passed the city-dwellers who were already growing accustomed to my daily walks. That solitary feeling intensified further when on bright mornings, farther down the leagues of islands and water that separated me from them, I could make out the hills of Entre Ríos where I had spent my childhood. But most of all, I missed the lively and stimulating company of Dr. Weiss, the long conversations at the table punctuated by constant sparks of his genius and humor; he was my true family, not because I renounce my kin, but because through him I discovered a new relationship, one that unites all those who, distinguished by their own traits that render dull the impositions of blood ties, look for new affinities outside those ties to understand and enrich these traits. And I can say that the only two moments of personal happiness I had during my stay in the city were the two long letters from the doctor, brought to me by the laborious detours of a most irregular post. In the first one particularly, the doctor explained that moving the patients could have been organized another way, a way not requiring my participation on the trip, but that he had chosen to send me so I might spend some time away from his side because, according to him, I was huddled too deeply in his shadow, and he wished me, as I carried out the risky and difficult task entrusted to me, to spread my own wings. Reading these generous lines, I was filled with pride and happiness, and I knew at last that the true teacher is not one who wants to be imitated and obeyed, but is capable of entrusting to his student, unaware until that moment, the very task he needs.

Aside from those two letters, which are with me even today, the little news that managed to enter the city had a common feature:

All of it was bad. The north and west, from which my patients ought to have finally appeared, if they were to appear at all, suffered only two or three ills—the rain, the cold, and the flood—but in the south, that is, in the direction we would travel as soon as we were ready, there was an additional scourge: Chief Josesito. With each new messenger his band's latest outrages were relayed to us in painful detail—never leaving out the inevitable violin concert over the human remains and tortured corpses. Hearing these stories, Osuna would wrinkle his forehead and suck deeply and more frequently at his cigar, biting it harder than usual. A few days passed before he would explain, at my insistence, of course, the cause of his restlessness: Because of the flood, the whole line of outposts between Paraguay and Buenos Aires had vanished; not only the Paraná, but all its tributaries had overflowed, so the lands were flooded well out to the west, which would force us to make a sizable detour northwest across open country before bearing south—or perhaps we would need to travel through high desert where there were neither outposts nor roads, and precisely where Chief Josesito was ensconced with his band of savage Indians. The bravery and expertise to lead us through open country were left to Osuna, whose brow furrowed not in fear, but rather in a professional and anticipatory concern, simultaneously considering how possibly to negotiate the obstacles on the road, of which Chief Josesito seemed to be the foremost. So it was that one morning, two or three days after our conversation, he declared that he was leaving to explore the surrounding area to see what turned up, and disappeared for a week. When he returned, the outlook was certainly not reassuring, but was more accurate than before he had left.

He had ridden first to the north until he met the covered wagons down from Paraguay. They were delayed but would arrive, by Osuna's calculations some five days hence, barring an accident.

Osuna then handed me a letter from a colleague of mine in Asunción, informing me of the presence of an additional patient in the caravan. The caravan's leader was to give me a sum of money to cover the cost of admission at Casa de Salud for one year. Osuna also told me of the covered wagons intended for the other patients; they were sufficient in number and everything seemed to be in order. He had also gone to meet the people coming from Córdoba. They were proceeding much faster because they traveled on horseback, but had been late to strike out from the city, though Osuna was ignorant as to the reasons why. They did not, however, seem to have a patient among them. It is true that their meeting was hasty, for Osuna had been heading south to acquire better information about Josesito. He had been unable to converse with them in greater detail, but they presented themselves as a small group of riders, traveling through the desert, careless and free, and whose leader, who looked to be a rich and magisterial man, but who had made some jokes about Osuna that the other riders greeted with laughter, had wanted to give him a few coins for the pains this man supposed Osuna had taken to come meet him. Osuna had turned them down and galloped to the south. It was plain to see that despite the offhand air he adopted while telling me this, Osuna had been annoyed and even a little humiliated by the horsemen's disconcerting breach of tact. And finally, passing into the south, he'd made inquiries about the movements of the chief and his band, and not only had he heard various testimonies, but had even glimpsed signs of a recent massacre: a pair of charred wagons, bones recently picked clean by tigers, caracaras, and ants. Such was the news Osuna brought me from his seven-days' ride.

In the nearly two months I stayed in the city, the cold relented slightly for just a few days to pass through a stormy corridor, from pale glacial weather, dry and sunny, to gray winter, biting and rainy. Day's brief hours passed in a wan half-light, and all the way out to the horizon, under a dark sky, everything one saw had a dull sheen, soaked through. On riverside streets, one could walk in the rain because the water had hardened the sandy ground, but in the western part of the city opposite the coast, a thin mud had stirred up, sticking to our boots, making it hard to walk; and one morning on a street in the outskirts, I saw a horse slip over and over, more precarious each time it tried to right itself, until it made a resounding flop on its side into the red and runny clay and remained there twitching its legs in the air to no avail while emitting strange noises—whinnies or wails—from either its throat or nose, though I could not tell which. At night, I could hear the rain, dripping thick and constant, or scattered and faltering as it abated, the sound reaching not only into my surroundings, but also to the vast night I imagined, spanning all the universe, so black and cold it seemed to come from beyond thought and sense, from a sudden place over and above the very space it pervaded.

One morning, two or three days after Osuna's return, Señor Parra came knocking at my bedroom door very early and in person: A man just in from Córdoba last night wished urgently to speak with me. According to Señor Parra, he seemed an important person by his manner of dress and—this he said in a bit of a huff, lowering his voice—was probably used to giving orders. From Señor Parra's tone, I knew the visitor had offended him in some way and remembered the story Osuna had told me about the horsemen, so I rushed to dress, as Señor Parra, who was usually affable and tolerant, seemed to have grown impatient with the visitor and would rather I received him as soon as possible. I looked to him gratefully, trying to make it clear how I regretted the disruptions that my stay in his house had caused, and invited him to enter; as I finished dressing, I inquired further about the character who had come so brazenly to take me from my bed at such an early hour on that dreary morning. Señor Parra put aside his pride and stoically overcame his ill temper, replying that when the servant came to announce the guest, seeming most impressed by this character, he had gone down to receive him personally at the front door. The visitor was dressed, said Señor Parra, with a meticulous elegance for that early hour and for that untenable weather, straight and stout and quite sure of himself, with a book in hand and his index finger between pages so as not to forget where he was reading; he had to admit, said Señor Parra, that the visitor left an immediate and forceful impression. He attributed the man's rather haughty manner to the shyness sometimes caused by strangers, producing a temporary arrogance that expresses less a suspicion of others than of oneself. Since he asked to speak urgently with Dr. Real—he had to consult him about a matter of the utmost importance—Señor Parra took him to his library at once, and, with an attitude that might have seemed discourteous, the visitor paid him no mind and began to examine the collection, now and then making assorted little sounds, which were difficult to interpret as approving or disapproving, and nodding his head, affirmatively for a second and then negatively or doubtfully. He was surely a man of science and, though his conduct may have been a bit indelicate, up to that point he had not actually given offense. However, when the visitor noticed the bust of Voltaire, he shook his head like a doctor at an incurable patient and, with a sarcastic chuckle, he let slip—involuntarily but with the rudest and most contemptuous of tones—the word *scoundrel*. That had been too much for Señor Parra to endure, and, announcing to his visitor that he was going to look for me, he had come knocking at my door.

We hurried out into the gray morning and crossed the cold, rainy courtyard (all the while, I was still adjusting my clothes), to receive the man who, I had no doubt, must be the peremptory associate from Córdoba, head of the band of strong and loquacious riders who had offended Osuna on the plains by offering him a pair of silver coins. I was determined to maintain a professional dialogue with the visitor, terse and stern, to punish him harshly for the breaches of conduct committed against two people whom I held in high regard, so before entering the library I carefully adopted an attitude which precluded all courtesy and familiarity—but on seeing me come in, the visitor spoiled my plans with a cordial, even enthusiastic greeting. Rushing to receive me, he briefly extended his hand, shaking mine energetically, and, after asking me if I truly was Dr. Real, told me that for months, ever since he'd begun correspondence with Casa de Salud in fact, he'd been eager to meet me and Dr. Weiss, who'd come with such admirable references. He was a tall, heavyset man who, but for a slight overhang of belly, had the build of a true athlete. Despite the encroaching fat, he still gave the immediate impression of physical strength, really an intangible life force, which was almost excessive. He must have been about thirty-five, so were it not for a few gray hairs that just whitened his clean, tousled brown hair about the whiskers and behind the ears, he would have been the very picture of a man in his prime. But there was something unstable in his manner of speech as well as his physical exuberance, and no matter how elegantly he wore his expensive clothing—a pearl-gray cape, the flounces of his shirt emerging in an impeccable white froth from a dark jacket, long trousers of light brown English worsted that disappeared into the legs of tall and lustrous boots, a slightly darker brown and of European make, whose aspect (no less immaculate than the rest) drew my attention and made me wonder how the devil he had managed to keep the leather free of mud, even near the soles—his whole person betrayed a sort of self-forgetting, as if the instant of dressing and preening so carefully before he came to call on us had elapsed into a past so distant and in a world so different from the one we were in now that it must lie dark and forgotten for all time, that the reality shared among all beings and things dated back no more than fifteen or twenty minutes. Our visitor, who seemed to feel a flamboyant regard for me, treated Señor Parra, who was barely able to hide his indignation, with deliberate condescension and spoke only to me; not only did he do everything possible to ignore Señor Parra, but he even seemed to calculate his every movement in order to keep his back to him at all times. As for his conversation, I must relate that the visitor began with a string of praises to my person disproportionate to the scope of my reputation, which was eclipsed, and justifiably, by that of Dr. Weiss, but then, and almost without pause, it became a professional (and even philosophical) examination; questions piled vexingly one atop the other, leaving me no time to answer— questions which our visitor, who interrogated me with shameless persistence, seemed to lose all interest in even as he asked them. This tense arrangement lasted some minutes, and even if I had not spotted the saliva bubbling at the corner of his mouth and the sudden fixity of his gaze, then the breakneck conversation, jumping from one subject to another with hardly any logical conti- nuity, and that sense of enthusiastic but situationally-inappropriate energy that emanated from his person, led me to see that I was not meeting with a colleague—rather, this was the Córdoban patient we had been expecting, which his accent confirmed. From his bearing, which indicated symptoms of mania, I was addressing none other than Señor Troncoso, whose family, one of the richest in Córdoba, had sent him to be admitted at Las Tres Acacias. A typical behavior in that type of patient is precisely that air of superiority assumed in the presence of their doctors, and the tactic of coming to see me without notice explicitly to ascertain my clev- erness or even, if possible, my total ineptitude—a fairly standard mode of presentation. In his face there had also been an attempt, skillful enough on his part, to conceal his madness, like a drunk- ard who, to avoid detection by others, tries to adopt the poses he believes most natural, never realizing it is those very attempts that betray his drunkenness. Señor Parra, unused to this manner of madness, looked more and more annoyed by what he believed was an extreme case of ill breeding, so I cast him a collusive glance, signaling him to calm down and, approaching our visitor, told him firmly to be quiet and invited him to sit. Though he obeyed, I saw from his excitement that it would not be so easy for me to pacify him. (Maniacal fits are characterized by a continuous excitation that builds to a crest and tolerates no interruption, not even sleep, and one of the symptoms that appears most often is, in fact, insomnia. In the throes of an attack, a patient can go several sleepless days without loss of strength, appetite, vitality. When it passes, the fit gives way to long periods of melancholy; during the attack, however, the steady increase of excitation can culminate in quite a frenzy.)

Although he remained seated for several minutes, Troncoso lost neither his verbosity nor his good humor, and, though he had no alternative but to listen to me, rather than answering my questions regarding the trip from Córdoba, their arrival, the escort accompanying him, the meeting with Osuna, and other things of that nature—questions which, unlike his, required precise responses that he did not seem disposed to provide—he chose to laugh at me like a child and, I must confess, as commonly occurs with certain rather talkative madmen, merely repeated, with a friendly and comical air, the last words of the last thing I said, or, making even Señor Parra laugh, proffered, as his sole response, words that had no logical relation to the last word of my sentence, but that rhymed with it. Such behavior, which might seem ridiculous to one who hears it described without ever having had occasion to observe it directly, manifested quite calmly, and Troncoso set forth precise sentences and rhymes. An unsuspecting person who entered the library in that moment might have believed that, before Señor

Parra's astonished gaze, Troncoso and I were playing a witty, pleasant, and otherworldly parlor game. After a time, Troncoso stopped and, as if he had grown bored of that very game (though not for the world did he lose the air of one passing a most diverting morning), he searched the room for some new distraction, returning his attention to the bust of Voltaire, and, with two vigorous strides, planted himself a meter from it and began to spout mockery in made-up French, which was largely composed of Castilian words spoken with a French accent, from which, now and again, there shone some *musié Voltérr.* For some mysterious reason, each time he spoke he would throw back his head abruptly, and with a haughty, contemptuous expression, he would toss his abundant mane, wavy and clean. Weary of that overlong performance, which had Señor Parra vacillating between bewilderment and rage all the while, I demanded that Troncoso bring me to the people who'd accompanied him from Córdoba, a demand he seemed not to hear, but he shook his head with a resigned and condescending smirk, and made his way to the front door. He was obviously hoping I would follow him and was acting deliberately, with that disdain the mad sometimes show when submitting to external reason without all the arm-twisting, feigning as if they were obeying the order more by coincidence than by the voluntary change brought about by reason. Present and vivid among all my memories thirty years later, Troncoso carries on as the very picture of the autonomy of madness—that to avoid apparent servitude to causes still unknown to us should be less caustic than the rather unjustified certainties of good health. As I wanted to see his escort, Troncoso took me to the street, and there they all were, seven or eight Córdoban horsemen mounted in the muddy street and squeezed beneath a couple of long military cloaks held over their heads to protect them from the rain. Their dark eyes gleamed in the half-light, a little denser than the gray air on that rainy morning, which thickened the capes' shadow about their faces. One of the men held the reins of the only riderless horse, a tall, blue roan, restless and energetic, and just as mysterious with regard to its general being and its deeper motivations as the man who had ridden it from Córdoba, and who had now pocketed his book in his pearl-gray coat and was preparing to mount again, taking not the slightest precaution to save the page he had marked with his index finger the whole length of our interview, but taking infinite pains not to stain his overly shiny boots with mud. Even so, I marveled at the agility, the ease, even the grace of that stout frame, in which I had noticed his incipient obesity and the white hairs that started to gray his well-groomed hair, as he leapt on tiptoe, so as not to dirty his boots, over the ground where the mud was runnier and stickier, and his neat jump was almost balletic as he grabbed the reins held out to him by a member of the escort and set his right foot in the stirrup, steadying himself on it to propel his leg cleanly over the back of the horse, which recognized its rider (perhaps from the weight, smell, voice, and style, or even the madness—or who knows what other distinctive detail) and received him by bobbing its head twice, as if in agreement, before growing motionless again, preparing perhaps to receive the order to break into a gallop. An obvious hostility emanated from Troncoso's escort toward me, and its members did not even try to hide it, unlike Troncoso himself, who had transferred that hostility to Señor Parra—the aforementioned having nothing to do with the matter—reserving for me an exaggerated regard in which irony and jocular self-assurance bordered on scorn. Of those men who had to protect him from so many external dangers (mainly, from those provoked by his own behavior), escorting him across the desert and into the hands of science to look after his health and try to return him to reason, Troncoso had formed a band of underlings, almost henchmen, who looked more like outlaws than caretakers; he clearly fascinated them, perhaps with that singular, radiating physical force that they were unable to understand, perhaps because the unruly excess had yet to present the opportunity. His obvious prowess enthralled them: tireless activity, physical strength, witty camaraderie, bravery, and, most importantly, the constant drive to renew that activity in a thousand different directions, many of which were contradictory and even mutually exclusive, based purely on his sudden and unpredictable changes of mood. Those simple men saw them as the features of a grandiose and magnetic originality, when really, in the eyes of medicine, they were banal signs, observed in nigh-constant repetition in a thousand different patients, foreshadowing collapse.

It became clear to me that I had to immediately impose my authority on the band of horsemen, their dark eyes scrutinizing me, undecided, from the shadow of the military cloaks that protected them from the rain; with a firm but friendly voice I asked who led the group, to which a man dismounted in silence and removed his hat, but didn't uncover his head, which was wrapped in a sort of red handkerchief tied at the nape of his neck, and made as if to hand me a leather pouch, but I ignored the gesture and asked him to come inside. Without inviting him to sit down, I had him spread the contents of the pouch onto a wicker table that stood in the hall, which consisted of several letters addressed to me from Dr. Weiss and some medical and financial documents. In the letter addressed to me, I was informed that the bearer of the same, which is to say the man with the red handkerchief, was a reliable servant of the Troncoso family, who desired that I allow him to accompany us to Casa de Salud as the patient's personal guard. Although it seemed an excellent idea to me (later events would prove my error), I pretended to think for a moment before accepting, and even permitted myself to explain to him, with exaggerated seriousness, the state of his master's health, advising him that, if he wanted to be part of our caravan, he must keep in mind that I was speaking of a mobile hospital and not a company of soldiers or ranch hands, and that in hospitals it was generally doctors who gave the orders. The man listened, unblinking. He must have shaved that morning, and he had the dark skin common to those who live and work in the elements. His fealty to Troncoso seemed to tug at him, and so did the convincing tone that lent my speech professional authority. If some doubt remained about the state of the man he was supposed to protect, subsequent episodes in our travels would do away with it. The man was loyal and well intentioned toward his master, but a little lacking in spirit despite his fierce freebooter aspect. His name was Rosario Suárez, but since Troncoso called him El Ñato, or Pug-Nose, everyone called him by that nickname. He had a dog-like loyalty to Troncoso, despite the fact that Troncoso often treated him with indignity, not out of madness but because of his role as master.

Four days later, the wagons arrived from Paraguay. Though expected for weeks, their appearance produced a great commotion in the city; they had been joined by several merchants and even a troupe of actors, so for several days a sort of fair took place on the edge of town where the caravan had settled, as the mud kept it from reaching the city center. The wealthy families traveled to the outskirts to do their shopping; two or three carts were down from Asunción, and one even from the Brazilian coast carrying goods that were commonly used, but terribly scarce in the cities of the Viceroyalty, owing to Madrid's trade monopoly over the colonies. In those years, one had to resort to contraband to access such goods; even the city merchants would come to shop and supply their own businesses. Ladies and gentlemen from town came to get a taste of the poor neighborhoods, accompanied by slaves bearing packages or holding up large umbrellas, black as the hands that clutched stoically at curved handles to keep them aloft over their masters' heads to protect them from the rain. A troupe of actors tried to enliven the atmosphere, but the weather was so bad that it became impossible to act outdoors, so they were finally invited to give a show at the Casa de Gobierno, where they performed a coarse and disjointed farce that, for some mysterious reason, garnered enthusiasm among the city elites and dominated conversation for days.

While it lasted, one of the main attractions amid the bustle was Troncoso himself, who found in that impromptu fair the ideal venue for his irresistible taste for performance, playing the role of an elegant, witty man, chatting with one and all, and so ostentatious he could not be missed. He had grown calmer shortly after our first meeting, perhaps when he realized, as the days passed, that I had no intention of being either his enemy or his assassin, and if his behavior was indeed rather striking, it did not seem to stray too far from the usual, and people regarded him as an entertaining and slightly extravagant man, whose strong accent told of his Córdoban origins. It was known that he suffered some vague infirmity, though his ceaseless activity must have convinced more than one that it was an unfounded rumor. He lived lavishly, which enhanced (obviously) the number of his admirers in the city's only inn. I called on him daily and we spoke amiably, barely touching on—and not without innuendo—the edges of his eccentricity, but when he saw me arrive at the fair, where he was having almost more success than the smugglers and actors, he would vanish discreetly, perhaps out of fear that I would assert my medical authority and humiliate him in public. By revealing that connection to reality, he eased my concern, though only to an extent; experience has generally proven that, beneath that deceptive meekness, frenzy often grows impatient.

This brings me to my two new patients, who, along with the guard that accompanied them and the other members of the caravan, had to negotiate an incredible series of obstacles to arrive in the city. The patient we were expecting, about whom letters had been exchanged between Asunción and Las Tres Acacias, was a man some thirty years old called Juan Verde, a relative of the owner of the transport company that had rented the wagons to the patients' families for such a reasonable price. The man would go from hesitant silence to overly-lively or impassioned conversation, which, oddly, tended to consist of a single sentence. He repeated it constantly, changing his intonation and adding such varied facial expressions and gestures that it was as if he were indeed holding a conversation with his interlocutor in which, as spoken sentences changed, so changed the feelings and passions that spurred them. To be clear, I should state that what Verde always said was not even a sentence, as it had no verb, but consisted of the expression *morning, noon, and night,* which he addressed to his interlocutor, and sometimes even to himself in the course of the conversation, always repeating it and changing only the intonation, which at each exchange would suggest such distinct things as greeting, courtesy, astonishment, joy, anger, disagreement, concentration, interest, et cetera. That curious form of speech, which ultimately wore on his interlocutors, as one might guess, alternated, as I have said before, with many hours of hesitant silence each day. As for the unexpected patient, I must admit that all his papers were in order when they entrusted him to me on arriving in the city. He was Verde's middle brother, son of the same father but not the same mother, and as he was much younger (he would have been fifteen or sixteen at most), all members of the caravan, to distinguish between them, and with certain affectionate familiarity, began to call him Verdecito, or "little Verde."

Since antiquity, many causes of madness have been posited, varying by the type of illness under discussion, and so, when multiple cases appear in the same family, not only in parents and children but even over generations—or as they seemed to occur in the Verde family, in the same generation—the suspicion that hereditary factors exist in certain cases of insanity seems more than justified. Without being quite identical, the Verde brothers' symptoms displayed many similarities, particularly in a sort of perversion of speech; it did not manifest the same way, but still drew attention. (Dr. Weiss noticed the phenomenon immediately, and he tried to make an inventory of the two brothers' shared symptoms, as well as their divergent traits, in order to establish a classification principle for both. I will not rest on these details too long because, as the reader will recall, the object of this memoir is not to enter into scientific minutiae.)

Verdecito, as we called him, might have been the finest young man in the world, but, owing to his symptoms, his company could grow exasperating after a time. This explains why, despite his docility, the family had rid themselves of him, sending him to Casa de Salud. In the letter they sent from Asunción, justifying the lad's unexpected delivery, they offered the explanation that the two brothers were joined so intimately and by such a deep affection that it would have been cruel to separate them—that perhaps neither one would survive. Accustomed to the oft-criticized rhetoric that families usually resort to in order to justify admission of any of its members seized by madness, I made haste to uncover the true source of Verde and his younger brother's continuous verbal, oral barrage—whatever you might call it—to which they submitted their interlocutors. The pretext of a cruel separation that neither would survive did not bear up, for I could show even the most incurious bystander how clearly the two brothers barely knew each other, speaking—or not speaking, to be more precise— to one another with the vaguest and most apathetic indifference. Verdecito, contrary to what transpired with his older brother, was able to maintain a fairly ordinary conversation, and his repertoire of phrases was varied enough, although their concepts and themes always proved a little childish for his age and, as if he

102

were slightly deaf—though he was not, and reacted immediately to other stimuli outside the conversation—showed a tendency, which could become exasperating, to repeat the phrases spoken to him several times. What hampered his verbal exchanges was his custom of continually making all manner of noises with his mouth: screams, grunts, sneezes, hiccups, coughs, stammers, belches, and, in moments of great excitement, profanities, and even howling and yelling, though directed at no one in particular. It was impossible for him to pass by a horse without neighing to make fun of it, or any other animal without imitating its cry. He did so with ease, and was sometimes given to copying even the other noises he heard around him, from a spoon's metallic clink against a tin plate to the murmur of water passing from one vessel to another. So it was that Verdecito's presence was always accompanied by an endless string of buccal sounds that were strewn throughout his sentences and, more importantly, filled the silences between them; perhaps the simplest explanation for that tendency to repeat the sentences uttered to him stemmed not from an alleged deafness, but from the fact that the constant din from his mouth simply blotted out the conversation. Leaving aside the exasperating aspects, it is worth pointing out that neither brother was able to maintain a normal conversation with people, in one case owing to his emitting too great a variety of sounds and, in the other, too poor; there was this paradox, that, in the one capable of offering such a gamut of sounds, his conversation seemed more apathetic, while the one who repeated his four paltry words ad infinitum seemed more emphatic. There was something poignant about those two brothers, separated from the world by the same impenetrable wall of madness; two different mothers had brought them into the world, so if it was hereditary, their insanity could only have stemmed from the paternal branch. Perhaps what they inherited was not madness but a shared fragility before the harshness of things, or perhaps, by unfathomable coincidence, the secret vagaries of fate had made each, though different from the other, traverse the same hidden corridor where, without brutality or compassion, madness lay waiting.

With my five patients, I felt like one of those circus jugglers spinning five plates by their rims on a table at once, dashing about from one plate to the next to keep them all spinning upright and at the same speed, never dropping or breaking a thing. All the while, the time of our departure drew near. We had yet to repair the carriages that had suffered damage on the rough roads, to assemble a few more troops to serve as our escort, and to see an improvement in the weather, so that a storm would not force us out into the desert, which was inhospitable even on clear days. By then, we stood at July's end, the dead of winter: not a leaf on the trees as they rose gray in a dark and shining filigree against the flattened sky, itself a gray that was ever so slightly brighter. The freezing downpours had given way to a steady drizzle, which, after two or three days, turned to a sort of mist that seemed always to float, motionless, between earth and sky. It seeped into things, icy cold, leaving them soaked to the marrow. Getting into bed, the damp, chilly sheets stuck to the skin, and no matter how the braziers burned day and night, not to merely heat the rooms but to speed evaporation of the damp, nothing was ever completely dry. Those milky, suspended water droplets filled every available space. The water was everywhere, falling not just down from the sky, but also creeping up from the region's many and powerful rivers as they overflowed; from the city center to the outer districts, it imprisoned the town in a watery ring that narrowed by the hour. Many houses built too far down in the lowlands had already flooded, and some riverside streets could only be traversed by canoe. The five or six thousand inhabitants of that forgotten desert village, which the official papers called with certain hyperbolic pomposity *a city*, kept watch on the water's height from the moment they rose each morning; the rest of the day, trapped in that air of imminent disaster, they spoke of nothing else. In those final days, the delay weighed on me too heavily: Little tied me to that place, though it was, in a way, the site of my childhood. Returning to that city after so many years, it was there that I first learned how the world that endures in the places and things we have left behind does not belong to us, and what we abusively name *the past* is no more than the bright but gauzy present of our memories.

At last, the day arrived. The rain ceased one afternoon, and the next morning the sun appeared in a clean, cold blue sky. The puddles froze over and, as the sun remained chilly, the ice stayed solid on the journey, changing color in time to the day's shifting hue. Everything had been ready for a week, and we awaited only that change in the weather; despite the frosty air lashing our ears and faces, we men and the horses were impatient to leave and pit ourselves against the plains. Even the mad, who always give the impression of being enclosed within their own order, apart from the outer world, seemed agitated by the prospect of the voyage. In Sister Teresita's eyes, the sparks of a malicious glee grew brighter and more frequent as the time for departure approached, and young Parra, prostrate and all that implies, seemed to have slipped from the stubborn rigidity that imprisoned him, and within just a few hours of setting off on our trip, a most curious phenomenon took place, which I will refer to in detail a little later. The Verde brothers' unusual traits intensified: The older one could always be heard shouting his unavoidable *morning, noon, and night*, punctuating it with endless outlandish gesticulations. But surely it was Troncoso who was most altered by the situation. He had hoped to lead the operation himself, and though most of the soldiers and cart-men already knew him, a few who didn't believed him to be the head of the caravan; I had to gather everyone two or three days before departure and explain, firmly, that only Osuna and I were qualified to give orders, and that Sergeant Lucero, who commanded the small escort, would join the two of us to make decisions once we were underway. That meeting cost me an indignant missive from Troncoso, who had summoned me the same day via his doting aide, Suárez El Ñato. I myself, as I mentioned earlier, was impatient to go. I had nothing to show from the slow and frozen weeks spent in the city, save the lasting friendship of the Parra family, who I took the opportunity to visit several times in later years due to young Prudencio's admission to Las Tres Acacias, and the pleasant evenings of inspired conversation with Dr. López, taken up almost entirely by professional matters.

We left, then, at dawn on the first of August, 1804. If anything, of the many incidents, difficulties, anomalies—or however you'd like to call them—that made up our travels—if anything, as I said, could sum up what was to come, perhaps the absurd fact that inaugurated our journey would be enough: Namely, while our destination lay to the south, our caravan started off north, and we had to travel that way for a few days before veering west to seek our true course. The party from Asunción had been forced to backtrack across the Salado River a bit farther northward, as it splits into two branches near the mouth, and both were equally flooded, turning the entire region into an expanse of water two or three leagues wide, rendering it impossible to make out the riverbed. When he came across the flood, Osuna had explored the field upstream to find a relatively dry patch, narrow and sandy enough for canoes to pass through. For that reason we had to first head north past the fork in the river, farther up the floodplain, to the winding places that stalled the current, and, after a less-than-easy crossing, bear west for a stretch, only then to return south, swinging parallel to the water several leagues inland. There, according to Osuna and others who knew the region well (though not quite as well as the usual post-road), without too much difficulty we would cross the endless line of streams, brooks, and rivers that cut across the plain from west to east and flow into the currents of the Paraná.

Although horses, not oxen, drew the covered wagons, we inched forward: First of all, in the wake of those steady rains, the state of the roads—if the winding tracks we followed in open country could be called roads—hindered our progress; but at the outset, our convoy was to have consisted of a fleet little group of carts to advance along the line of outposts that hugged the river, a few leagues from one to the next, until at last we reached the white building at Las Tres Acacias ten or twelve days later. However, I must admit that our convoy instead became an unwieldy caravan, lagging and long, slowed by perpetual indecision like a clumsy, hesitant snake, whose belly and tail each fancy themselves as much in charge as the head. I do not mean to say that any one member of the convoy, sound of body and mind (if, under the circumstances of our crossing, such a phrase still held meaning), tried to replace the deliberative triumvirate formed by Sergeant Lucero, Osuna, and myself, to which we sometimes added an Indian who accompanied the troops. Rather, I mean that in such a large group of people, thirty-six altogether, everyone's desires could not very well go hand in hand at every moment of a journey that announced itself from the start as lengthy and difficult.

Apart from the six wagons, one for each patient plus my own, driven by cart-men from the transport company that would return them from Buenos Aires to Asunción with different cargo, there were two more carts designated for our needs en route. One was a sort of grocer, general store, and galley, whose proprietor, a Basque man who had spent years trekking across America, had actually made a living from his mobile warehouse. As he told me one night, he would accompany troops of soldiers, merchant caravans, or simple travelers to Brazil, Paraguay, or Santiago in Chile, from the other side of the mountains. He had all manner of wares in his cart, which had a raised side-panel supported by an iron rod that hooked around to the opening's lower edge, which could tilt over the outside almost like wings, leaving real shelving and a narrow counter in view, over which he sold *yerba mate,* sugar, sponge cake, brandy, wine, tobacco, thread, buttons, and much more, or if those wouldn't do, on the counter were an assortment of drinks and bits of cheese or sliced meats. In one corner of the wagon he had his bunk, and a little mirror hung on the wall where he would take pains to shave every morning. Many in the region, and likely in the south of the continent, knew of him, and according to Osuna, he'd grown rich from usury. In the other cart traveled three women who first had me believe that they were the wives of three soldiers who always brought them along on deployments. Once the trip was underway, though, I realized they were prostitutes, and that the three soldiers who had been passing as their husbands were common pimps. Sergeant Lucero explained that such women following military companies on the plain were a common sight in the region, and that sometimes they might really be wives, or even both at once. Resigned to how easily I'd been duped, I thought how what perplexed me would have charmed Dr. Weiss, as that wife-harlot combination the sergeant spoke of was, in a way, the incarnation of his ideal woman. One of the three was French, and blonde to boot, and she stood out from the other two who had dark skin, high cheekbones, straight black hair, with aquiline features that made them look so much like serving girls or, if you prefer, like Egyptian queens and goddesses. Despite her fair hair and skin, it did not initially occur to me that such a woman might come from France, but she overheard me correcting Troncoso's abysmal French one day and approached me with the unmistakable accent of the Parisian working-class. This was a curious experience for me, as the words she uttered felt out of tune with the countryside, even as they gave me the chance to practice the language of Rousseau and Buffon in the middle of the desert. She came to my cart several times to relay the wild adventures that had led to her current situation, but after two or three conversations the versions began to differ, so I doubted their truthfulness. Our bond was broken altogether when one day, on the fourth or fifth visit, she hinted that she was actually working, and that I ought to pay for the time we had spent in my cart as if such visits were professional ones. That shameful moment could have incensed me, but it became clear that, though outward circumstances do indeed shape our lives, there is always something within us that makes us lose sight of those circumstances and colors them with our perceptions—and our perceptions, though we never realize it, are tarnished by pure delirium. (Speaking of those three women, I must say that they were trounced on their own ground by Sister Teresita; she visited them often at first, but they came to spurn her for what we might term *unfair competition*. My French confidante came to tell me one day that she'd stumbled onto the little nun with two soldiers, lying among the grasses some distance from camp. She was aghast, shaking her head and repeating at every turn: *Tous les deux, monsieur, tous les deux! Ce n'est pas malheureux?* When I told the story one night back at the Casa de Salud, Dr. Weiss laughed, remarking: *One of the most surprising aspects of theology is the prodigious work theologians do to elaborate a system that has at its foundation an unutterable experience. Saint Thomas suspended the composition of the* Summa Theologica, *after all that sweat, the day he finally had a genuine mystical experience. Such an important fact as the certainty of the existence of the divine can dispense with any commentary. Theology, which is essentially political, troubles no one. Mysticism, on the other hand, is empirical theology, and I've always thought its practical application capable of sowing panic in the Church, in the Court, and in the brothel.*)

Our escort was made up of sixteen soldiers, with Sergeant Lucero to command them, and the Indian, Sirirí, a docile Mocoví whose two primary traits, I would say, were prudishness and hatred for Chief Josesito; the mere mention of him in Sirirí's presence darkened his face. The more unreasonable demands of the Catholic Church, which at that time were not taken seriously even in Rome, seemed to have found in Sirirí the proper soil to take root and flourish to the point of caricature. He did not drink, smoke, curse, nor swear in vain, and it suited him to cross himself on any pretext and kiss a little gold medallion that hung around his neck. Sergeant Lucero, who valued him because he was in fact a trusty guide as well as an interpreter, said—when Sirirí was not around, of course—that as a boy he had swallowed a catechism and had yet to finish digesting it. When he spoke of Chief Josesito, Sirirí's hateful expression became so disturbing that one began to feel kind toward the musical murderer, who, by contrast, at least displayed a certain humanity when he was drunk or set to playing the violin. Sirirí's principles, strict as they were, suffered many grueling tests over the trip, during which there was not only prostitution, alcohol, and violence to weaken his moral foundations, but also the addition of madness to dash the walls of the doorless, windowless building in which religion had caged his wild and fateful soul. Osuna, who was like two different people depending on whether he was drunk or sober, respected him by day for of his knowledge of the desert and loathed him by night.

We were a diverse and colorful convoy: One part of the escort went before us and the other brought up the rear. My carriage came at the head, and those of the five patients followed behind, then the Basque's warehouse, and finally the women's wagon. Of the carrt-dwellers, only Troncoso and I traveled by horse, he on his tall and skittish blue roan, so tense and lively it was nearly always reined in and ready to break into a gallop at any moment.

It seemed also to have contracted its rider's strange ailment, held in a state of exaggerated activity, morbid and unceasing. The escort soldiers did not wear uniforms, but dressed more capriciously, and though several tattered, faded military garments had made it into that ragged assemblage, the diversity of the rest ultimately caused it to lose all unity. From that haphazard motley, diametrically opposed to the careful design implied by the uniform, which seeks repetition, order, and symmetry, no doubt gave off an equally lively effect, especially from the colors and designs on the ponchos—solid, striped, dark or light, fringed or unfringed—that, in the desert's empty space, seemed to take on additional clarity, especially in those early days, when they swelled in the icy southerly wind or fluttered over the backs of their owners. The wagons shone dimly at first, too, as they had been cleaned, oiled, and partially repainted with the company colors by their own cart-men on their arrival from Paraguay. Following the last of the soldiers, a herd of fresh horses went meekly, driven by the horsemen who would take turns at the task. And, finally, ten or twelve stray dogs followed us with the same stubbornness, need, and eagerness as seagulls trailing a ship's wake in search of sustenance.

As a doctor, my primary responsibility was, of course, to busy myself with my patients, but as Osuna hinted, and I came to understand, the posture of a leader or master was expected of me, so I locked myself in my carriage to ponder how I might display that posture more clearly, concluding that the best way was to underline the fact that it was I who paid the expenses for our expedition, though I later realized that those ragged mercenaries we called our escort—some of whom barely understood a word of Castilian because they came from Corrientes and Asunción and their mother tongue was the native language, Guaraní—expected me to make the necessary decisions about the direction of our unusual caravan. As it was impossible for me to carry out that duty without Osuna and the sergeant, I decided to adopt a distant and thoughtful attitude, delaying my response to their proposals and pretending rather to weigh the *pro* and *contra* of each before making a firm decision. I must say my farce yielded a far better result than expected, since the one who seemed to have the most doubts about my abilities, which is to say Osuna himself, turned out to be the most gullible of all. Many years later, he would still speak of me as a man of the plains, though never in my presence. In reality, I do not know if my authority prevailed because the wages were paid in the promised amounts and terms, or thanks to my professional reputation, for I was able to treat all the maladies those rustics endured over the long month of our trip with my little valet case of medical instruments and emergency remedies. Colds, diarrhea, scrapes, boils, insect stings, fever, back pain or hemorrhoids, or else old complaints, already bound to the bodies of their victims, flared up with the bustle of the trip, and not a single day went by in which one of those *gauchos*—thirty years later I use this word cautiously, although I know it has lost the somewhat insulting sense it had in those days—did not come to my carriage, embarrassed but helpless, to consult me.

We had barely left the city when, as I have prematurely mentioned, the evolution of young Prudencio Parra took an unexpected turn: I had found him completely prostrate in his bed, fist gripped tightly, gaze fixed upon the void, deep creases on his forehead and between the brows to give him that suffering and lifeless expression, and this gave way to a certain animation—as I dare call it only in comparison to the months-long, total stillness—whose singular feature was the series of movements he made with his hands, repeating them incessantly, even at meals, which he absorbed meekly and indifferently. He would sit up in his bunk, and, unbothered by the jostling, would begin his movements, which he could replicate for hours like a machine, every so often casting a slow and serious glance at his hands, followed by the faintest of sad smiles.

He would extend the fingers of his right hand and then slowly contract them, until it gave his hand the look of a claw, though soft and never threatening; after a brief pause he'd continue the same movement until he closed his fist completely. And finally, when his fist had been closed for several seconds, his left hand would cover it and squeeze it hard. All day long, whenever anyone was present (since, mad or sane, it is difficult to know how a person acts when he is alone) he would make those gestures. While they surprised me at first, I came to think of them before falling asleep, and I realized that they were familiar to me, and, though I did not know why, this brought to mind the arcades of Alcalá de Henares one sunny spring noontime, giving rise to an agreeable sensation in me. When I woke the next morning and my mind, locked at night by the keys of sleep, opened to wakefulness, the first thing that awaited me was the answer to that mysterious sense of familiarity: In philosophy, we had studied Cicero's *Academica*, and as the exam period drew near, I went strolling down Alcalá's main street with a friend, memorizing that page where Cicero describes how Zeno the Stoic showed his disciples the four stages of knowledge: Fingers extended signified Conception (*visum*); when he folded them in a bit was Assent (*assensus*), by which Conception becomes patent in our spirit; then, with closed fist, Zeno tried to show how, by way of Assent, one arrives at Firm Conviction (*comprehensio*) of said Conceptions. And, in the end, raising his left hand to his fist, enveloping it and squeezing forcefully, he showed that motion to his students and told them that it was Knowledge (*scientia*). On remembering this, I leapt out of bed, and having dressed myself summarily, barreled down to young Prudencio's wagon where he, in that early hour, was asleep and peaceful-looking. His open hands rested palms-down on the gray poncho that covered him.

The Paraguayan soldier who had been an army nurse, and as such was entrusted with the care of the Verde brothers, and whose duty it was to look after the patients with another of his comrades, had ably tidied up the bunk. Again I noticed, as I had already several times in his home that, judging by the state of his bed each morning, young Prudencio's nights must have been restful indeed. I stayed, hoping he would rouse himself, for I was keen to observe him pass from sleep to waking, to see how the strange machinery of his hands would set itself in motion. After a long time, he rasied his eyelids, as was his custom, and if my presence startled him he made no sign of it. He sat up slowly in bed, eyes hooded, and, resting his back against the carriage wallboard, began to stretch out the fingers of his right hand, preparing his left in the air so that, when the first three movements of the cycle had been completed, the fourth, in which he covered his right fist with his left hand and pressed forcefully, might be performed. The points of the two ever-present bits of white cloth stuck out from his ears, for whenever anyone tried to take them Prudencio would howl piteously, forcing me to order his release. But the impressively sunken area from cheekbone to jaw, the recessed cheek, had filled out somewhat, and his face, still so pale, looked unquestionably rounder and healthier. As was customary, he made as if to ignore me, but something told me that, from the remote location where he had been inwardly secluded for several months to escape the tumult within himself and in the world, the remnants of his self, abandoned perhaps in the blackest corner of the universe, were broadcasting signs of life. That his movements were completely identical with the gestures that served Zeno the Stoic to enact the phases of knowledge for his disciples (according to Cicero), I had not attributed *a priori* to some inconceivable coincidence between the ravings of a sick boy and the imagery wrought by the father of the Stoics at the height of his faculties, as if logic and madness might arrive at the same symbols by different roads—which can happen more often than one might think—but rather attributed it to the more easily explainable fact that in his period of avid and haphazard reading, young Parra might have one day encountered in a paragraph of Cicero, immediately making it his own, the explication of that inextricable world in whose disorder his fragile mind, astonished and terrified, had been awakened without knowing why.

But there was something yet more curious in young Parra's sudden, if slow and limited, activity. It continued to hold my attention, and I took note of it in light of that golden rule which Dr. Weiss had instilled in me: According to him, all of a madman's actions, as trivial or absurd as they seem, are significant. The fist that Prudencio held closed stubbornly and forcefully for so many months, which he only deigned to open from time to time so that his nails might be cut (and not before snatching up an invisible breeze with his other hand using the same gesture, though a little gentler, as we make to trap a fly in the air), that fist that had taken the strength of several men to open after so much time, had relaxed for some mysterious reason once our convoy left the city, and his two hands had begun to effect the precise but unhurried movements I have just described. As I believe has also been said, because of the flood we had to go north for two days until we met a bend in the river shallow enough to let us cross, so that, once on the opposite shore, we could journey in the other direction along the river's western bank, returning, so to speak, to our point of departure. That situation gave me the opportunity to confirm the most surprising detail in Prudencio's behavior: Since his fist relaxed as we left the city, once we started to approach our original point of departure before veering west to trek through the desert, would his hand-movements cease and his fist close up once more, its strength apparently renewed? While we kept to the outskirts of his native city, as we had plotted our route, his fist tightened obstinately, but the moment we began to seek dry land to the west, his fist relaxed, his body straightened in the bunk, and the hand movements, which had been so familiar to the students of Zeno beneath the Athenian arcades two thousand years ago, brought to light by unexpected means, promptly returned. A single explanation seemed possible to me: Every unique but fragmentary place in the world is embodied in its totality, so for young Parra, his birthplace contained the universe in all the enigmatic complexity he had tried to decipher with the help of frenetic and chaotic reading, until one day he lost his mind. So, as we moved away from the scene of that destructive experience, the terror diminished, but when we drew near it again, proximity to the city, steeped with such a painful past, caused it to worsen. (*To this philosophical explanation of Doctor Real's, let us offer a simpler and, more importantly, likelier counter: that what moved away and came closer with the trip's ups and downs, and what had driven that poor young man mad, was not the enigmatic universe or anything of that sort, but, as is patently obvious, his own family.* Note, M. Soldi.)

It has already been noted that, to reach a latitude nearly equivalent to our starting point, we had to travel four days, which under normal circumstances would have been a quarter of our journey. And so, as the fifth day dawned, we started westward, determined, searching for the dry land that would allow us to go south. Within hours, we advanced into the flattest, emptiest, most wretched part of the plain. A southerly wind, frigid and persistent despite the limpid sky—not a single cloud in sight—pummeled us across our left flank as we made our way inland, shaking the dried grasses along the ground, winter-thinned and gray. We traveled all day, bearing away from the water into high desert, and when we camped at dusk under a low sun—enormous, round, and red, almost touching the horizon's edge, accentuating contours with a brilliant red halo—I had the impression, more sad than terrifying, that we had arrived at the very heart of isolation. Above the lowlands slipping quickly into the night, it seemed to me, for a few moments, that we were the only living things to writhe beneath that crushing and disdainful alien sun. I probed all along the circular horizon with my gaze, detecting no other motion but the trembling inclinations of the wind-whipped grass, no sound but the whistling of that icy blast from the south. And though I knew the desert swarmed with life, not just animal but solitary, nomadic human life, it was the inhuman wind in that landscape that made me shudder. Never, not before or after that journey, have I received, as if I were ruler of the barren land, the enormous red sun and, some hours later, the overwhelming stars, such clear tidings about the true state of all things growing, creeping, fluttering, pulsating, and bleeding, twitching in grotesque contortions, within the fiery engine that, for some reason, chance had placed in motion. We lit a modest fire, as brush was scarce in those parts, and, after we ate, I got into bed partly-dressed to ward off the cold and, before falling asleep, read a few pages of Virgil by candlelight.

For leagues and leagues, in every one of its parts, the desert remains identical. Only the light changes: The sun recurs, rising in the east, climbs slow and regular to its zenith and then, with the same ritual precision with which it has reached the apex of the sky, descends to the west and, finally, having grown enormous and red, gradually fading and cooling, flaring with a brightness perhaps familiar in infinite space but foreign here below, then sinks to the horizon and disappears, covering everything with night's viscous blackness until, a few hours later, it reappears in the east. Were it not for the changing light and color of that perpetual turning, a rider crossing the plain would think himself to be always riding in the same point in space, in a futile, slightly oneiric sham of motion. (On cloudy days, that illusion is perfect and a little unsettling.) The rhythmic sounds of displacement—in cart, in carriage, on postal coach or horse, repeating and identical for long stretches, despite the regularity, if not the absence, of the terrain's features—seem also to infinitely repeat the same moment, as if time's colorless ribbon, stuck in the groove of the wheel (or the who-knows-what that displaces it) shimmers motionless in place, suspended and unable to rest because of its essence of pure change. Such monotony numbs. As a rider moves forward, things might often happen that are specific to a place, but they come to adapt themselves to that illusion of repetition; if at first they succeed in attracting the traveler's gaze and even his curiosity, past a certain point they become more than familiar and float, phantomlike, far outside experience, and, at times, even beyond knowledge. The life that swarms among the tall, even grasses, for example, pulled out of their quiet by the passing of a cart or horseman, that diverse and vibrant life that could occupy a naturalist's whole existence—the traveler with no other concern but to leave behind those poor, abandoned fields as soon as possible might find his interest awakened at its first appearance, but after a few hours it blends into the most uniform monotony. If a hare leaps into his path, his eye will always capture the same image of the jump, and he will always see the short-tailed hindquarters a little more sharply than the rest, springing up, while he will just make out the tips of the ears in a flash as the head dives into the grass. In the case of partridges, it will always be a pair, plumage neither gray nor green nor blue, and with a metallic sheen, that comes flying side by side, male and female, almost level with the grasses, to disappear into them again and take up their short, slow flight on a light breeze a few meters away. League after league, the same caracara will appear, wheeling over the same skeleton, and the same wild horses on the same winter migration will graze in herds of fifteen or twenty, tiny and docile, along the horizon. A peculiarity in the scenery that suddenly appears, introducing diversity, repeats itself over the leagues and ultimately there is nothing but the same field as in the beginning, a field whose novelty fades almost at once. Like the sea, the plain varies only at its edge; its interior is like an undifferentiated nucleus. Barren and measureless, when it produces some imperfection in itself, that imperfection always gives the illusion (or the perhaps the true impression) that it is the same one, again and again. When something out of the ordinary happens, its passing is so intense and vivid that, whether brief or lasting, its evidence will always seem too much, and will trouble us.

Thirty years later, when I recall that trip on rainy nights in Rennes, I often think: No one in the world knows what loneliness, what silence is, but me. One morning, ten or so days after departure, I broke off from the convoy with Osuna and rode about an hour to explore the surroundings on the pretext of visiting some ranch, which, at any rate, we never found, and to this day I suspect was purely imaginary, and that the real cause for our excursion was Osuna's growing fear that, any day now, we would come face to face with Chief Josesito. It was not the loss of life he feared, but rather his reputation as a guide; as his task consisted of bringing us safely to our destination, he too would find himself vulnerable if he failed. It was near ten in the morning, and as the south wind had died down and not a cloud appeared to block the sunlight from warming the earth, despite how recently the first days of August had passed, a herald of spring was already drifting in the air. The brightness grew so quickly in the clear morning that Osuna and I seemed to be galloping not to somewhere on the horizon, which appeared motionless and always set in place, but to the impossible point in time where the noon hour shone, flaming and fixed. At the edge of a lake, we paused to let the horses drink and I saw that, due to spring's premature beginning and the terrain's favorable saturation, a new flower was beginning

119

to sprout. In order to observe it, that I might discuss my findings with Dr. Weiss later on, I proposed to Osuna, if he promised not to be long, that I would wait for him by the lake while he finished exploring the surroundings. Osuna was flattered by the interest that spot awakened in me as if he were its proprietor, accepting my suggestion immediately, and with his habitual bent for practical matters that, to one who did not know him as well as I, might have concealed what tugged at him internally, flew straight into a gallop southeast. He went clear and deep into the morning, and his green-and-red-striped poncho flowed about his rigid torso, angled back somewhat, shrinking by disjointed leaps as if he were being compressed, and when he'd gone far enough that hoof-beats could not be heard, the motion of the gallop—without the accompanying sonic consequence to grant it intelligible sense—became an unreal caper, almost impetuous, like that of an exaggeratedly loose-joint-ed paper doll manipulated via an invisible thread, tossing about silently in the air until it collapses to the ground, undone. Osuna and his horse, still distinct from each other only because my mem-ory persists in saying so, after that clear compression by successive leaps, became so small that before the horizon swallowed them up, all at once, with no transition, and disappeared, and no matter how the eye went searching for them just over the horizon, there, in the dark and insignificant strip of land under the open blue sky, endless and even, like a luminous abyss, it could not catch sight of them again. Although the mind presumed that they remained, it could discern no indication, no sign, no consequence of their presence or their passage.

 I stayed alone by the water. The crested screamer birds, espe-cially the lapwings, showed their distress at my arrival with loud, insistent cries. They came and went nervously across the shore, passing by without even seeming to look at us, a-shriek and a-quiver, ruffling their plumage as if trying to rid themselves of the threat our presence posed. Ever since we crossed the river north of the city and began to advance through the plains, we saw many different animals in larger numbers than usual, and, in the case of several species, in places they were not in the habit of frequenting. That strange profusion was due to the flood, which had covered vast expanses, driving many animals from their usual habitats and forcing them to settle on the strips of dry land. In this way, we had seen a bloated, muddy undulation of alligators moving west along with the water's edge, and an uncommon quantity of felines that, though they lived amongst the trees and undergrowth, had to migrate to the open plain to escape the waters. As we passed through the lowlands near the flood's western border, however, plants and animals were found in their customary places once more. The animal abundance was easy to notice, and the unchar-acteristic presence of certain species arrayed on terrain they were not in the habit of frequenting gave the traveler the impression that upheaval had produced a sort of disorientation, of disquiet, or even panic, in the animals, which made them forget their ancestral postures and, taken from that immemorial form, allowed them to live on what land remained as they waited for the world to resume its normal course. The presence of so many different species in such a confined space—creeping, scampering, swimming, or flying, standing motionless in the water, or winging through the air—gave the countryside a motley aspect, with the arbitrary disposition of examples in a naturalist's engraving. Since childhood, animals have often seemed to me like painted things, perhaps because it has been impossible to put myself in their place, to imagine what hap-pens within them and, simultaneously—except perhaps for dogs—because we inspire a sort of indifference in them, present in the bird flying high in the skies just as in the horse we ride or in the tiger that prepares to devour us. Beyond their outward actions for survival, they are inaccessible to reason; it is easier for us to calculate the movements of the furthest star than to imagine the thoughts of a dove. A group of butterflies that all unmistakably perform the same motion at the same time puts our categories of *individual* and *species* to shame. Few understand the meaning of the word *precision* if they have never seen a flock of birds coast above a field in the crystalline evening sky, accurate and swift, tracing the same varied figures in unison. They are smaller, no doubt, of a shorter and more limited lifespan, but they are more perfect in and of themselves than man, who is clumsy and incomplete. And amid the loneliness of the plains, their unreachable external appearance of painted figurines is further intensified, rendering them almost ghostly. The hare that leaps into the rider's path and disappears into the grasses seems at once to be and not be, both real and present to the senses and a fleeting phantom to the imagination.

The lapwings that came and went noisily on the shore of the lake, realizing perhaps that their screams were not going to scare me away, grew quiet and disappeared into the brush to stand guard at the nests they had built on the ground. For a few seconds, there was no living presence before me, although I knew that life was teeming in the water, on the banks, and in the surrounding countryside. The lake, some fifty meters in diameter, reflected the blue of the sky, lightening a little from mixing with the water's beige, acquiring a sallow, and, in stretches, slightly greenish tint. Light from the high sun flickered on the surface and when some movement, however small, came to disturb it, a fleeting sparkle, slightly more intense, flared and faded several times, and then, quieting, mingled once more with the constant and uniform vibrations rippling the water. There was nothing outside myself but the lake; the near horizon, so round it looked as if it had been drawn with a compass; the winter grasses, still gray, in which spring shoots could not be perceived at a distance; and above, the dome of the sky like a blue porcelain bell, supported at the base by a circular rim that fit the horizon's circle to the millimeter, where the incandescent stain of the sun, which I was unable to see as I was facing west, where Osuna had disappeared at a gallop, was growing hot at my back and neck through my jacket. I was still mounted on my horse, which trembled, perhaps awaiting an order, motionless, hot and sweaty. I clapped a few times at its own damp neck and back, which it received with repeated head movements and, unsaddling, I took a few steps to the lakeshore, bringing it by the reins to quench its thirst. It lapped up water peacefully for a time, almost delicately, and then, seeming satisfied, straightened its neck again and looked into the distance, perhaps at the line of the horizon that curved smoothly beyond the lake. But, as I believe I've said above, the horse made it difficult for me to know exactly where it was looking and to infer thoughts (or however to call them) from such calm, visited periodically by the disturbance of nervous quivering, gentle and distracted as if the horse did not suppose it was living in its own body. I peered intently at its profile, and, as if warned, it did not turn its head toward me once, with such apparent stubbornness that it seemed to purposely treat me with indifference. For a second, I had the unmistakable impression that it was putting on and then, almost immediately, the total conviction that it knew more of the universe than I did, and therefore understood better than I the reason for the water, for the gray grasses, for the circular horizon and the flaming sun that glistened on its sweaty hide. With that conviction, I found myself all at once in a different world, stranger than the ordinary one, in which the outer world was unfamiliar to me, and so was I to myself. Everything had changed in a flash, and my horse, with its impenetrable calm, had wrested me from the center of the world and expelled me, without violence, to its edge. The world and I were separated and, for me, would never be quite the same again from that day forth; as my gaze strayed from the horse and alighted on the blue water, on the gray grasses, seeing the enclosed capsule resting blue above the horizon with us inside, I realized in that new world, born before my eyes, it was my eyes that were unnecessary, and that the expanse of strange countryside, of water, grass, horizon, blue sky, flaming sun, was not meant for them. The silence was utter, and every sound heard against it, small as it might be, could be heard clearly in each of its disordered parts: an animal gliding among the grasses; my own breath; even the beating of my heart, a sound that a fire beetle seemed to suddenly mimic in the distance; the horse's muffled and curious snorts as it tossed its head, abstracted. An absurd notion came to me: I told myself that, exiled from my familiar world, and within that boundless silence, the only escape from terror was to disappear myself—that, if I concentrated hard, my very being would sweep that world along with it into nonexistence, that world wherein I was beginning to glimpse the nightmare. But my consciousness rebelled, persisted, whispering: *If this strange place does not drive a man mad, then he is no man, or he is mad already, for it is reason that engenders madness.* On that beautiful, sunny morning, panic began to set in when I saw a tiny dot begin to grow on the southwestern horizon, its movements hazy at first, then taking the shape of a man on horseback, until I saw the blaze of Osuna's red-and-green-striped poncho, and a few minutes later Osuna himself reined in his horse three meters from mine and told me that he had thought the better of it, and had decided to come back to find me so we might make a larger turn without having to pass by the places we had already explored along the way. (Months later I told Dr. Weiss of the impressions I had during the few minutes I was alone with my horse at the lake. The doctor's expression grew serious, and he reflected for a time before answering: *Between the madmen, the horses, and yourself, it's hard to know which are the truly mad. We lack a suitable perspective. As relates to the world you live in, whether strange or familiar, the same*

124

problem of perspective presents itself. It's true, though, that madness and
reason are inseparable. And to the extent you point out the impossibility
of knowing the thoughts of a hummingbird or, if you like, of a horse,
I want to note that the same is often true with our patients: They do
without language, or distort it, or use one for which they alone hold the
meaning. And so while we want to understand their performance, we
find it's as inaccessible for us as that of a speechless animal.)

As we speak of madmen, it seems to me I should proceed with
the memoir and return to my own: They were my chief concern,
and of course, with the obstacles standing in our path, placing
them safe and sound into Dr. Weiss's hands was more complicated
than I had imagined. Of the five, I knew there were three who,
even if their illness were to worsen suddenly, would not cause further problems. Locked within the narrow cells of their madness,
they seemed to have dispensed with the outside world altogether,
and any aggravation to their state was not going to make the prison
where they lived darker or more wretched, nor increase their indifference and passivity. The elder Verde's monologues, passionate
as they were, were not meant, at heart, to convince anyone, and
Verdecito's mouth-sounds were a sort of sonic wall that cut him
off from the world—not to mention young Parra who, some mere
months after he was admitted to Casa de Salud, allowed himself, without complaint, to be taken out of bed for the first time
(and a year later, out of his room). As exasperating as he was, the
elder Verde's only phrase—*morning, noon, and night,* as you will
recall—with which he tried to address every theme of conversation, argument, and even fatherly edification of his interlocutors,
was enacting the paroxysm of his madness, and a change of state
could only reduce his fervor to the deepest gloom. With regard to
Verdecito, it is true that hardship increased his anxiety, his mouth-
concerts, and his deafness—I had to repeat the most trivial phrases
several times before they reached him—but as far as what I speak

125

of, the main trouble was that he stuck to me like my shadow and seemed only to feel safe at my side, which on one hand allowed me to monitor him, but on the other would cause me to lose patience and, as a corollary, disturb his calm.

It was Sister Teresita and Troncoso, even prior to departure, who worried me. Unlike the others, they grew unruly because, as often happens with a certain class of the mad, rather than shutting themselves in, they fervently believed in the legitimacy of their delusions and wished to impose them on the world at all cost, militant in their madness. The little nun was convinced that Christ had ascended to divine love in heaven after the resurrection, separating himself from mankind, leaving only his sparks scattered among men. She, then, had as her mission to reunite these sparks through the carnal act, to merge divinity and humanity anew. Her *Manual for Love* is exceedingly explicit on this point, and though her thinking disintegrated in the final pages, giving way to a senseless list of profanities, there is a reasoned exposition of her doctrine in the first part of her treatise, which, if one briefly adopted her theology's point of view, is unassailable indeed. Given that theologians call purely speculative and rational theology "positive" and mystical theology "negative" (I believe), we can imagine that, drafting her *Manual*, Sister Teresita, like Saint Thomas, acquired her conviction to enact the recommendations received from Christ in Upper Peru, and if this hypothesis is true, it casts new light on the *raison d'etre* of her treatise's final section. In any case, Sister Teresita was without the slightest doubt a troublesome presence in our caravan, and the central dilemma she posed for me was trying to keep her apart from the soldiers without imprisoning her in the wagon; there was a contradiction between keeping her under lock and key during the trip and the fact that in Las Tres Acacias, the patients, with very rare exceptions, could move in total freedom throughout the establishment. Another problem was knowing to what extent the members of the convoy—cart-men, soldiers, whores—were aware of the sort of madness that had taken hold of Sister Teresita. For the first two or three days I held the illusion, completely unjustified of course, that nobody knew of the little nun's erotic ravings until, one afternoon, I saw a group of soldiers in a circle near Basque's saloon, looking profoundly attentive and serious as they listened to somebody speaking inside. Intrigued, I approached to see what was being discussed, and over the shoulder of one of the soldiers I was able to confirm that Sister Teresita, slit-eyed with indignation and lowering her voice, as if disclosing a terrible secret, was revealing to the soldiers that, *If Christ was crucified, it was because he had such a huge . . .* and accompanied her words with a familiar gesture, raising her hands to chest height and, placing the palms facing each other some thirty centimeters apart, bobbing the two simultaneously to indicate an approximate size. When she saw my astonished face over a soldier's shoulder—he, like all the rest, was bewitched by Sister Teresita's words and failed to notice my presence—the nun began to laugh, and with an impudence that makes me smile to this day when I remember, stuck out her tongue, ran it with feigned delight across her narrow lips and, preempting my summons, left the circle of soldiers and accompanied me meekly to her wagon. We never discussed it, and it all happened casually, but what impressed me most deeply, and especially incited me to reflection, was the seriousness, even the gravity, with which the soldiers listened to her. It was clear they would not doubt for a single instant, for the rest of their lives, that the little nun had just revealed the true cause of the crucifixion.

Regarding Troncoso, the complications that brought about a change in his condition proved much more serious, even endangering the life and property of the members of our caravan, demonstrating once again, though such redundancy is needless, that delusion, whether the philosophers like it or not, is as qualified—if not more so—as the will to direct the order of events according to one's whim. Even before departure I saw Troncoso's agitation grow, almost imperceptibly at first, manifesting in an unspoken grudge against me that drove him to compete with me, especially for the organization and command of the caravan, a responsibility which, as I believe I have said, I shared with Osuna and Sergeant Lucero. Ever since I had to display my authority before him and his men during our first encounter at Señor Parra's house, Troncoso's feelings toward me had vacillated between dread and spite, prudence and mockery, respect and resentment, forecasting the difficulties that often follow the aggravation of hostility, and which were to multiply on a journey like the one we were about to attempt. But despite his ill-concealed disdain, a disdain to which I doubt I dissuaded him from adding both sarcasm and slander, he was my patient, nothing more, and as I was his doctor, his health and his person were my responsibility, all of which would come to naught unless I could incite him to more moderate feelings. When we were still in the city, Troncoso always assumed, in a manner perhaps vaguely deliberate, an attitude that bordered on the limits of my tolerance, for I, as his doctor, instructed him in our daily conversations in what he was allowed to do as far as his comings and goings, his public conduct, his meals, hygiene, and daily routine, though, as I have already said, he was always on the verge of disobedience. The moment we began our journey, his fiery temperament grew rather more flammable, and I feared (and not without reason) an explosion at any moment. His remarkable animation, which lacked an object in the monotony of the plains, kept him from staying at rest in the wagon as the other patients did and, no matter the hour I went out into the morning after rising and getting dressed, he was already mounted on his blue roan, trotting about nearby, talking loudly with the soldiers or cart-men, who did not always seem to quite understand the meaning of his sarcastic remarks, or his shouts and orders. He was a gifted rider who went about as though he had forgotten he was on horseback, but he never committed a single fault; the beast he rode seemed indifferent to its rider, as well, and all they did together—walk, trot, gallop, race, halt, reverse, or prance—seemed the result, not of an undetectable order given by man to beast, but of a spontaneous and almost magical coincidence that, by extended chance, externally harmonized the casual movements of two wills, each focused on itself and ignorant of the other. His expertise as a horseman overcame the soldiers' reservations, and, despite his eccentricity, they grudgingly respected him, which, along with El Ñato's obsequious loyalty, complicated my monitoring duties. A sure sign of his worsening state was that he not only engaged in frenetic activity without any practical purpose all day and night, since he barely slept and gave no sign of weariness, but also the fact that his external appearance—his clothing, beard, and mane of hair—was deteriorating, for he hardly changed clothes or shaved anymore, let alone bathe. As a result, his trousers and jacket were riddled with stains and even holes, and his flounced white shirt, so clean on his arrival in the city, was all wrinkled and of an uncertain color. There were always a few little bubbles of saliva foaming at the corner of his mouth; if anything contrasted with his body's restless fever, it was the steadiness of his gaze, shot through with veins that clouded and reddened his eyes. Sometimes at dusk, he got down from his horse and walked stiffly among the motionless coaches with great, energetic strides, chest puffed, head erect, hair disheveled and skin browned by the sun—a sun which burned a little brighter each day. He might have a book in his hand, poring over it without breaking his stride or, if he left off reading (or pretending to read), he did not deny his thoughts externalization with shouts, hoots of laughter, or condescending and garbled observations that he would direct to whatever member of the caravan he encountered, not stopping as he passed. A few times, he visited me to demand I modify the trajectory which, according to him, would help speed the journey, but mostly he complained about the three prostitutes and the nun—whom he dubbed, with a caustic smirk, *the Strumpet Superior*—present in the convoy, claiming the contract his family signed to stipulate the conditions of his treatment would feature prominently within the clauses that the patient was not to mingle with persons of low estate or dubious morals. He sent El Ñato to me daily with a dispatch, which I, obviously, never answered. Sometimes his nonsensical proclamation went on for several pages and sometimes was limited to a single sentence that might have seemed to be gibberish at first glance, or to have many different meanings upon successive readings, or, if one remembered later and thought the better of it, a precise but enigmatic meaning which, though the reader had divined it himself, was impossible to unravel. Troncoso saw those continuous ravings as a grand political program destined to change the foundations not only of society, but of the universe. According to those proclamations, he was to depose the King, disown the Viceroyalty, guillotine the Roman authorities, and also—I transcribe this last claim word for word—*to abolish, once and for all, having no other basis beyond custom and the spiritual enslavement of the peoples, the hereditary and unwritten privileges of the Sun and the other stars in the sky.* The construction phase of his program consisted of federating the indigenous tribes on the continent and, to avoid giving offense, bestowing them with a ruler from outside their ranks and who was also to play the role of supreme representative of a new religion, a kind of king-priest to impose legislation on social and religious life, at once military commander and spiritual father of the new community. Needless to say, for anyone able to decipher his bulletins' tangled prose, the traits of this eminent personage had more than one point in common with the author,

130

borne increasingly along by his delirium to envision himself as the legitimate master of the universe. He was beside himself when I left his messages unanswered, but it would have been a mistake on my part to grant him the slightest sign that his ravings could be taken seriously. In his defense, I must admit that in my long life, in Europe just as in America, in recent years, I have seen the same insanity as Troncoso's succeed many times. Thanks to the reading of Tacitus or Suetonius in the painful centuries that came before, such insanity prospers now until it reaches its foolish objectives, which are none other than crushing, on pure whim and overweening pride, with bloodied heel, the hopes of the world.

The truth is that even to the most careless observer, Troncoso's mental state was worsening day by day, hour by hour. He was barely sleeping, and it was useless to try to lock him in the wagon— it only enraged him—so I chose to release him under the watch of the nurses and myself. On his own, he needed ten times the attention of the other four patients combined. He had adopted the custom of apostrophizing the rising sun each morning, pacing back and forth on a short imaginary line, always in profile against the red disc as it rose slowly from the horizon, and addressing it, shaking raised arms in its direction without looking at it directly (he tried it several times, but always at the noon hour, so it was impossible to gaze for long—he would grimace, face darkened and flooded with winding trails of sweat that soaked his shirt at the neck and back). When the convoy set out in the morning, he would mount his roan and spring ahead in a gallop until he almost disappeared on the horizon, but immediately we would see him return, the horse's slate-colored coat crackling with sweat, veins bulging and body throbbing. His agitation seemed to increase with the heat, which, in those days—it had been more than fifteen since our departure—could drive one to distraction. On one hand, everyone marveled at Troncoso's wild ways and, on the other, at the horse's tolerance, forced, in that harsh and unbearable climate, to submit to its rider's every nervous start. There are many who think madness contagious: If so, it is less because those who surround a madman take on those same symptoms in his presence than it is because madness is so corrosive as to alter those who must coexist with it, bringing out their own symptoms which would have lain dormant in ordinary times; as that alteration results from neural pathways, but without the intervention of the will or reason of those afflicted, it would not be so strange if Troncoso's horse had gone mad just from living with him. The truth is, an event took place in this already-delicate situation that, though we had feared it since before departure, we would rather not have had transpire: Some travelers had come across the followers of Josesito, or whomever he was, and the tragic circumstance of discovering their remains fell to us.

It was a fresh massacre, four or five days old at most, but almost nothing was left of the six bodies that lay strewn across the camp. Chimango caracaras and crested ones, and black and red-headed vultures pecked at wild dogs in dispute over the abandoned remains; the big cats, already sated, had stripped them almost completely, leaving bones and bits of hair and fingernails, and now swarms of black and red ants were busying themselves with ungainly and stubborn speed, with the dried filaments that the packs of stronger, faster animals had deigned to leave, having come out of nowhere and then vanished once more. The Indians had left whatever they could not carry to a beast fiercer than all the others: fire. A great circle of ash interrupted the unending pastureland, marking the place where the bonfire had burned. Digging about in the ash, we found several warped pieces of iron and a few chunks of wood, all blackened along one side, where the embers had formed, and thus crumbled easily in the fingers. The bones were already bleached by the morning sun, save for those parts near the joints where strands of flesh still remained and where, accordingly, the ants were seething. In three or four days the bodies had reached, from the net of tissue and blood where they once struggled, from the constant pull and throbbing of doubt and passion gnawing at them, a freedom from the grueling chicanery of the particular and reached the immutability of universals through the white simplicity of their bones, passing first from subject to object and now, rediscovered by human eyes, from object to symbol. As we buried them, though several soldiers did cross themselves, it occurred only to the Indian Sirirí to pray, but his eyes were blazing as he did. Doubtless, the god he addressed must have been a double entity able to receive both his humble prayers and his raging thoughts; Josesito's crimes seemed to reach a part of Sirirí deeper than compassion or morality, home to a humiliation opposite to the chief's; if Josesito could not endure the Christians' arrogant superiority, perhaps what Sirirí could not support was feeling that he could not truly be one of them. That symmetry contained an irreconcilable antinomy, and I am sure that Josesito would have met Sirirí's hatred with the most violent disdain.

But it was Troncoso in whom our tragic find seemed to produce the strongest effect. Possessing a conscience apparently confused by its inconsistencies even as they perceive their interlocutors' skepticism, oftentimes the mentally ill try to put on an appearance of normality, only contriving to give their observers an impression of pretending, even theatricality. Though common to many patients, that impression was considerable in Troncoso's case, and the corpses of the poor, murdered travelers intensified it further. Though he avoided the burial, he tried to enact his mounting agitation by any means, as if warning us that our terrible find obviously confirmed all his absurd beliefs. He kept his distance but did not refrain from aiming reproachful, if not disdainful, glances at us, to which he added a determined expression that figured exaggeratedly in his features, as if to send us a message. On the plain's boundless stage, mounted sweaty and gesticulating on his roan, skin darkened on the parts of his face that went uncovered by his disheveled, white-streaked hair and beard, he looked like one of those bloodthirsty romantic heroes who, exaggerated by the artificial means of stage machinery, might shock an overly-credulous public in the theaters of Milan or Paris. And as he was not unaware that the word *delirium* is derived from the Latin verb for *to leave the groove or track*, that same night, supported by El Ñato's conspiratorial coddling, Troncoso put that etymology into action.

The very next morning, on his master's orders, the obedient Ñato came to give me Troncoso's last message. His irregular and ostentatious script had filled two whole pages at full tilt with incoherent stupidity, outlining his absurd ambition to go out to meet Josesito and talk him into unconditional surrender, thus helping federate the tribes of South America into a single independent State. When I finished reading these febrile insanities and looked up, indignant, I could sense El Ñato watching me with a malevolent and satisfied air, and by his expression understood that he and Troncoso had managed to evade my tyrannical watchfulness at last. For a few seconds, I lost control of myself in a fury and, forgetting my obligations as a civilized man, I seized El Ñato by the shoulders and shook him so violently that his red neckerchief, perhaps poorly secured due to the early hour and his rush to bring me Troncoso's bulletin, slipped back and fell to the ground, leaving bare El Ñato's completely bald head. The surprise disoriented me for a few moments, and as my shouts had begun to attract sleeping folk to my wagon and because it was El Ñato's baldness, more than my rage, that drew stares from the newcomers, there was a comic reprieve in the tragedy, and in the expressions of several I thought I glimpsed the brief thought that it was his baldness that had caused such a scandal. (Dr. Weiss asserted that pure tragedy exists only in the domain of art, and that in reality, even in its most appalling aspects, one always finds it tempered by some comic element, grotesque or even ridiculous.)

Consider my situation: A family had entrusted us with one of its members, a patient, for whom Dr. Weiss's Casa de Salud represented the last hope for recovery and I, having kept him in my care for a few weeks, had let him escape my watch in open country to go meet with a band of savage Indians. As he had twelve hours' lead on us and we knew that he and his horse were impervious to fatigue, it did not seem overly pessimistic to think he had already caught up with Josesito and his men, or that the Indians, with the same instinct as animals who unerringly surprise their prey, had already sensed the presence of a stranger in the barren land and had pounced upon him. Guarded by a ten-soldier escort, Osuna and I went in search of him across the endless plain, where a hint of spring had greened the grasses over the past two or three days, but an unseasonably scorching summer was already beginning to yellow them. During the days of our search, it was not Troncoso and his roan that we expected to find, but the rider's bones, already bare and sun-bleached in the lonely countryside. When, for all his expertise, Osuna lost the trail, it was through his patience that he picked it up once more, several hours later. But Troncoso's crazed energy, transmitted down into his mount, seemed to multiply the hours of our disadvantage. While we were condemned to rest, borne as we were upon poor human bones, they seemed to travel on the magical wings of delusion, which no obstacle of space or time can resist, and which would impose its outlandish and stubborn laws before crashing against the rocky indifference of the outer world. As the hours and days of search continued to accrue, my fear of not seeing Troncoso alive again grew stronger each time the traces of his movements dropped away, though they always reappeared; at last, now convinced that there could be no other possible ending, it took all my effort, as we galloped, dreary, across the soporific desert, not to let apathy defeat me: Such is the force with which that deserted land, once traversed, destroys all that we had accepted as familiar in ourselves before entering.

Finally, on the fifth day, the trail was fresh; Osuna tracked the blue roan's hoof-prints, and we began to search the surroundings. The tracks led us to a grove with some felled trees about a quarter of a league away, just at the western horizon, and so we concentrated our forces, refreshed by nightly rest, and cleared off in that direction, no longer at a gallop but a sprint, hoping, at least, that fatigued after riding almost five days straight, Troncoso had laid down to rest a while in the shady trees, protected from the blistering sun. When we entered the grove and had to slow our race to find a path without injuring ourselves among the trees, we did not see Troncoso immediately, but a clamor from the other side of the grove signaled his presence. Trying to stay quiet so as not to frighten our quarry, we set off down the path, still taking care to stay within the grove so as not to expose ourselves to whatever might be waiting on the other side. Just as we caught sight of the land outside from the grove's inner edge, we were able to attend the most unexpected exchange, and even I could say, the most surprising scene I have witnessed in my long life—and it is easy to imagine that due to my profession, there has been scarcely a single day that does not put me in the presence of something unusual.

Troncoso stood haranguing a semicircle of mounted Indians who were listening to him, motionless and fascinated. As soon as we glimpsed them, I realized the scene must have been going on for hours. Not far from there, the blue roan, tied by the reins to a clump of grass, munched calmly as could be, apparently indifferent to its rider's imperial designs; if, like Caligula, it ever occurred to

Troncoso to appoint his horse minister, it seemed quite likely that the roan would have disdainfully refused that so-called honor. The horse's indifference contrasted with the profound attention that the Indians paid Troncoso; he, however, did not even look at them, but paced back and forth in the same straight line parallel to the diameter of the semicircle, with an attitude similar to the one he would adopt each morning to apostrophize the rising sun. The Indian in the middle of the semicircle of riders carried a violin strapped across his back, and I recognized him immediately by the instrument of his hazy legend, and also because, of all those garish and ragged Indians, the attention reflected in their faces was profoundest in that of Josesito, who, as it happens, projected a rare intelligence and thoughtfulness, elbow resting on his horse's neck, cheek in the palm of his hand. In the five days of his frenzied flight, Troncoso's aspect had deteriorated further, and the only thing that still shone in his body, blackened by sun, dust, and grime, were his bright and bulging eyes, blazing enormously wide in a face almost entirely consumed by his dirty, matted hair and beard, which gave him the look of a wild animal, as if with the loss of his reason he was losing all his human attributes as well. From being put to immoderate use by its owner, his voice seemed to have gone hoarse, and as the meaning of his words did not reach us, from a distance it resembled barking or howling or the deep gutturals that preceded any known language. There was also a kind of alarm in the Indians' attention, and I understood its significance almost immediately when Troncoso veered abruptly from his straight line, turned, and approached the half-circle of riders, stretching out his arms and running toward them; this caused a general stampede among the Indians, who galloped away in a frightened clamor. Having covered a few meters they stopped, and, observing Troncoso from a distance—he had also stopped but kept up his blustering—returned to form their half-circle with the chief in the middle. Troncoso recommenced his back-and-forth on an imaginary line, straight and parallel to the diameter of the Indians' semicircle, causing them to stiffen up and begin again to listen to him with profound attention; the interest his words seemed to awaken in them had not yet erased all the terror Troncoso had etched upon their faces in the moment he had tried to approach them. They remained still once more, as Troncoso went back and forth, tracing the imaginary line with his steps in the grass, and his hoarse voice sounded in the silent morning air like the final dispatch from the world of incoherent creatures, hopeless and mortal, to the unfathomable and capricious law that had, one day, for whatever reason, set that world in motion.

The Indians were well armed and had slightly greater numbers, but, had we wanted a fight, our surprise attack would have doubtless been decisive, as they were absorbed, listening to Troncoso with some sort of poorly-disguised emotion, a mix of fascination and dread. That wild beast, hardened without and within by sun and insanity, rambling about and howling a hoarse, indecipherable harangue, weakened and gesticulating, seemed to hold for them the fascination of those mysterious things whose existence enriches thought and imagination, but whose contact, even briefly, withers and destroys with its lethal singularity. Hidden among the trees, irresolute and paralyzed by the surprise of what we beheld, we were able to watch the same scene repeat itself three or four times, or namely, that Troncoso, turning abruptly from his imaginary line, would open his arms and make as if to run at the Indians, slightly raising his hoarsened voice, and the Indians would race off to disperse in a terrified clamor, but a few meters farther out, when they realized that Troncoso had stopped and began to make a new line as the back-and-forth of his strides crushed the plains-grass, not moving forward, they returned to form up in a half-circle and, still slightly shaken by emotion and from dashing

138

off, again drew near to the pacing and, keeping a safe distance, again stopped to listen to him with dread and devotion, and even with reverence.

Both Osuna and I wanted to avoid a scuffle, not for lack of courage but because, if we lost, such a blow could lead to disaster for the entire caravan. I was also restrained by several scruples, primarily of a moral order but also of a legal one, for it seemed to me that, firstly, it does not fall to civilized persons to take an eye for an eye, and secondly, there was nothing to indicate Josesito and his men were responsible for the very real slaughter we had found, and as such a surprise attack would have been tantamount to execution without proof of guilt. These scruples mattered little to Osuna; like Sirirí, he had made up his mind, and despite the conflicting rumors that circulated about the chief, Osuna thought Josesito a cruel and cowardly murderer, though with characteristic good sense, he felt our objective was to arrive safe and sound at Las Tres Acacias and that the chief and his men were a matter for the authorities, in whose efficacy he, for his part, did not believe. And so we decided the following: Osuna and the soldiers would remain hidden among the trees, ready to strike, and I would go alone to collect Troncoso in the hope that, as he had been obedient until the moment of flight, even cursing and against his will, that in a last glimmer of conscience, he would obey once more. I brought a straitjacket with me but trusted it would not be necessary to fall back on, for I would prevail on Troncoso by my authority alone.

Once the soldiers were spread among the trees ready to intervene if needed, I set out at a trot into open country and made for Troncoso, keeping watch on the Indians as I did, so that eventual violence on their part would not take me by surprise. But just as the Indians ignored me, so did Troncoso. On hearing my horse's hooves, a few Indians had glanced in my direction, but almost immediately—and without the slightest gesture to show they had

139

noticed my presence, as if I had gone transparent—they went back to immersing themselves in rapt contemplation of Troncoso, who did not even seem to have seen me, though I cannot confirm this because experience has shown me many times how difficult it is to know the precise sense that the mad have of reality, which explains, as I believe I have said, that for many people madness and pretending are nearly synonymous. The fact is that when I arrived some thirty meters away, curbing my horse and trying to hear Troncoso's hoarse and lengthy discourse, I could not manage to make out a single intelligible word in that endless, animal noise, thinking that what was incomprehensible to me had to be yet more so for the Indians, who were returning, inexplicably, to their trance. After a few minutes, Troncoso deigned to notice me and, forgetting the Indians, came toward me with his rigid strides, very much like those of an automaton I had seen once in Paris, and stopped two or three meters away to launch his guttural harangue at me, angled slightly and not looking at me directly, but I could see by his round, wet, bulging eyes that he was already completely gone from this world. Having confirmed this vacancy, and faced with the fascination of the circle of motionless horsemen that contemplated him, it struck me that the Indians' interest was focused less on Troncoso's spectacular agitation in the apparently real world we shared with him, than in the report he brought us, stranded as we were in our gray, monotonous place, of the new and distant world that he alone inhabited.

Dismounting, I chose to leave Troncoso gesticulating alone behind my back, and I approached the Indians, my steps calm but resolute: I had already realized Troncoso was the best protection we could rely on. I made directly for Josesito, less for reasons of protocol than out of the curiosity his legend piqued in me, and as I spoke with him, discreetly studying his person, I was reminded of a time in a public garden in Montmartre when I had tried to observe an actor, celebrated all throughout Europe, who had been walking toward us just then. Physically, Josesito scarcely differed from the rest of his men, but his gaze, blazing with a provocative arrogance, was livelier and more intelligent. At first his Castilian seemed poor, inserting lots of infinitives and gerunds into the conversation, but soon, realizing I was losing interest in his agenda, he proceeded to speak correctly. When he caught me peering at the violin strapped to his back, I saw a spark of ill-concealed vanity in his eyes, but he pretended not to have noticed. And when he proposed to escort me to the caravan, I understood that he wanted to make it clear that he was aware of all our movements and had been perhaps since the very day we had left the city, but there was no shadow of threat or bravado in his insinuation, proving he was a realist. He already knew a group of soldiers waited in the clearing, and that I had already realized that as long as Troncoso and the other madmen were with us, the Indians would never attack because of the holy terror the mad inspired. Just in case, I went forward to inform him of the waiting soldiers in my most diplomatic tone, so that he would not take it as a threat and feel obliged to respond, and I summoned them, so they left the grove and approached at a trot, implying by their posture that they came with no intention to fight. The look exchanged when the chief and Osuna came face to face had that charge of the suspicion and hatred of mortal enemies who know each other intimately but who, for the moment and by chance, cannot unleash their violence. The Indians and soldiers seemed to measure one another with their gaze, each considering to himself the strangeness of the situation in which they found themselves. Or perhaps, prepared to destroy one another, each having forged a mythic image of the other, now face to face and obliged by an unexpected turn of events not to fight, they found the men a few meters distant to be all too real, different from the myth that they had forged. Ill at ease with respect to the possible duration of that exchange, I thought a quick retreat would be the most reasonable thing, and so I took Troncoso by the arm; he had lowered his voice and now, instead of haranguing the universe beyond until he screamed himself hoarse, he seemed to mumble truths to himself, each more fragmentary and dubious than the next, and permitted me to lead him calmly to the roan. The blue roan was placid, nibbling the bright green, tender grass, drawn back out with stubborn persistence by that mistaken spring from the flat, gray earth of winter's end. Busy selecting the freshest, juiciest little leaves from among the ravaged spoils of the previous year, the horse was utterly indifferent to the group of humans as we negotiated nearby, and if its indifference was justified in the general sense, it had something of ingratitude, and as I believe I have said above, of disdain as related to Troncoso. The knot of demented energy that had brought him there, in his heedless thirst for action, consumed him and then sputtered out, ultimately transforming him into a man who had housed an explosion, a sort of scruffy, blackened scarecrow, and the horse persisted in ignoring him, seeming to refuse to recognize his decline. Perhaps I had misunderstood the excited stage of his madness, and now he was arriving at the inevitable melancholy that, once the fire stopped burning, would have ultimately prevailed within that withered, worn-out husk. In fact, the previous days' near-magical fusion of rider and horse, during which they had seemed to form a single body, did not recur when, with my help, Troncoso settled onto the blue roan's back and took the reins. Each was buried in the depths of himself and seemed to have forgotten the other after whole years of communion. When we set back off, I galloped at Troncoso's side the entire time for fear he would collapse, but over the days of our return, he stayed rigid on the horse, preoccupied and quiet, and obeyed my orders with almost childish docility. The

Indians followed us the entire first day and a good part of the second until, around three in the afternoon, for the same inexplicable reasons they had come following at a discreet but regular distance, they abruptly disappeared.

Our arrival at camp mid-afternoon on the third day was received with happiness, especially by the soldiers who had feared by the length of our absence, though without transmitting their concern to the civilians they protected, that they would never see us again. When they sighted us coming up from the horizon, the bugler went running to fetch his instrument, and though he began by first sounding the regulation cry, as we drew near he intoned popular melodies and all sorts of musical jokes that conveyed to us at a distance, before verbal communication began, their relief at our return. The widespread disapproval won by Troncoso's escape turned to pity when the members of the caravan saw the state he returned in, and his physical decay was so eloquent as to make explanations unnecessary. They had readied the wagons in a circle to prevent a possible Indian attack, and if by any chance we had been delayed two days longer than expected, they would have held the course without us. As they were camped near a lake, the second we got down from the horses we ran to take a plunge, while some of those who had stayed hurried to slaughter a young heifer they had caught with bolas nearby, and which they had saved for our return. It was a celebration indeed, lasting almost until dawn: raucous, merry with liquor that the Basque, to general astonishment, distributed for free, and we sang and danced in the sultry night by the light of a great bonfire, all of us tiny and laughable, trapped in the triple vastness of the countryside, the night, and the stars. We were the effervescence of what lived—grasses, animals, men—and so we added to the endless, neutral expanse of the inanimate, coexisting through the colorful, tragicomic lightness of delirium in a multiplicity of worlds, each one closed-off and singular, wrought according to the laws of illusion, which, are of course more rigid than the laws of matter.

Naturally, once I refreshed myself in the lake, my first task was to examine the patients to learn what state they were in after eight days of separation. Broadly, mental patients belong to one of those categories that learned men of every era have tried with more or less luck to classify, as the diverse fluctuations of their individual states are rather unpredictable; and while external causes may affect their behavior, as has been proven many times already, it is difficult to predict or even clearly judge *a posteriori* the circumstances that might exert a real influence upon them. The truth is, in my eight days' absence, the patients had shown not a single outward sign of improvement or aggravation, and that stability, observed in numerous cases of melancholy, caused my dear teacher Dr. Weiss to ask himself several times if, apart from an acute attack (like that of Troncoso, for example), it isn't the greater stability of the former that distinguishes the mad from the sane. I must note however that I left them in the charge of two military nurses, whose efficacy also contributed to maintaining that stability.

A few hours after I examined them, during the celebration, I could tell that the camp's apparent tranquility concealed more than one conflict, and that the most reprehensible outrage came from those who were seen as "normal." After dinner, the French woman with whom I had spoken two or three times at the start of our trip came to inform me of certain things that had transpired in the camp during my absence. While her word did not seem entirely credible, owing to the many contradictions I had noticed when she told me of her own life and the reasons that, according to her, she had been forced to practice her profession, the facts she related, as outrageous as they might have seemed at first glance—and perhaps exaggerated out of jealousy and perhaps also from a feeling of professional indignation—seemed likely enough: According to the woman, Sister Teresita (caught by the same woman previously rolling about in the grass with the two soldiers) had engaged in sexual congress during my absence with *all* the men who had stayed in the camp, except for the patients, Sergeant Lucero, and the Indian Siriri. According to the woman, every night the soldiers would take turns entering the little nun's carriage, and during the day they invited her to drink with them in the Basque's shop. They were always together, according to the woman, and one or two nights, the nun had slept out in the open, splayed on the grass among the soldiers. A handful, five or six in particular, were glued to her side and acted as if they were her personal escort. During the day, since they had nothing else to do but hope for our return, the soldiers would go hunting on the far side of the lake to amuse themselves and try to find something to eat besides dried meat, and she would go with them, a cigar between her lips so she was always pulling faces. According to the woman, the little nun, in view of everyone, would step away and, lifting her skirts to the waist and opening her legs, urinated standing up like a man. Those details, more than her hedonistic activities, were what caused me to credit the Frenchwoman's story somewhat, for I had already observed Sister Teresita's tendency to take on masculine behaviors as if, in her endless search for the fusion of divine and human love, she also wanted to reunite the two sexes within herself. The loathing the little nun inspired in the woman who told me, irate, what had happened in my absence, was honestly the result of a misunderstanding, for the little nun's actions also included her, and it had to have been when she started to preach the Gospel to the city prostitutes that the idea came to her of putting into practice the order that was, according to her, received directly from Christ in Upper Peru in such a fashion. In one sense, instead of evangelizing the women of ill repute, she had been evangelized by them, and what the women took as an affront on the little nun's part, was, in a way, an homage she paid them.

To gain some clarity, I extricated myself from the woman, promising to handle the matter, as her rancor extended to the monetary side of things, and I went to see Sergeant Lucero. The slightly confused excuses I obtained perhaps proved that the French woman had not exaggerated, but when I called on him to show his usual sincerity, he confessed that he believed the rumors to have a grain of truth, but with all the soldiers implicated in the matter, it would be difficult to get the necessary clarifications from them. More than taking advantage, the sergeant told me, the soldiers seemed to protect and even obey her. He conveyed the sense that they quite revered her, though he knew not why; it was not she who instilled obedience in them, but they themselves who practiced it spontaneously and out of a deep respect that she seemed to inspire. Lucero was reasonable enough to see that the little nun, excellent person though she was, was mad, and that my medical obligation was to try to cure her of her madness and not to allow for half the world to become involved, and so we agreed to prevent, in the remaining days of travel, those unsavory complications from repeating.

The following day, after the celebration, it was laborious setting off, for at midmorning the soldiers were still asleep in the shade of the carts, as they had calculated the shadow's morning path before turning in at dawn. No calculation of that sort had been allowed to the horses, and they lacked even a lone tree in that vast, empty space to seek protection in the shade. In the region, it is said that the San Juan summer reaches its peak intensity during those days. It had arrived gradually, in the early days surreptitiously melting the built-up frost from the first icy week after the rain and, as it warmed the earth and air, had evicted the impatient plant-life, a fleeting simulacrum of spring. From the gray ground, hardened with cold, the new grass began to sprout, greening the flatlands, but after just two days, almost within hours, the heat grew and so the tiny leaves began to flag, and the fields dried up again almost at once, transformed into a vast, yellowed expanse. For days we saw not a single cloud in the sky—a deep and troubled blue—nothing but the blistering sun, leaving earth, air, and everything exhausted and hot, and because no wind stirred, and the nights were as hot as the days, nothing had time to refresh itself. We crossed that great furnace in the coldest month of the year, a huge yellow circle we trekked through at such pains, locked beneath its blue dome with only the sun's arid stain to travel it by day, blackened by night and filled with shining points, and for days it was the only scenery, so identical in every one of its interchangeable parts, that sometimes we were fooled into thinking that it had us bound, completely immobile. Movement seemed impossible past a certain time of day, but, as Osuna said, it was just as unfavorable to wait for dusk to travel when it was cool, first because to remain in the middle of the countryside, where we had no shade beyond what the wagons provided, was more grueling than travel, as our displacement might procure us some gust of air, laughable as it was, and in the second place because it did not cool sufficiently by night, but if we camped, the darkness, placing us under protection from the glaring sun for several hours, helped us to rest. With the heat, the silence of the empty countryside seemed to grow, as if all the species that populated it, unable to move, lay spent and lethargic. We too, who claimed to reign over them all, went about as if in sleep, men and women, civilians and soldiers, believers and agnostics, erudite and unlettered, mad and sane, made equal by that crushing light and the burning, brutal air that rubbed out our differences, reducing us to our equally feeble sensations. Shut in their wagons, the patients dozed all day and barely peeked out at night, save the little nun, who was always surrounded by her guard of soldiers, many of them almost completely naked, scarcely a pair

147

of tight and tattered breeches to cover them from the waist to just above the knees, and which left visible through their holes certain parts of the body that would have been more prudent to keep hidden, giving them an indecent appearance—though no one took notice, and it even seemed respectable compared to the women, who, when it was hot enough, walked about with their breasts bared and sometimes completely nude. When we passed by a river, almost everyone undressed without even waiting for darkness, and went to frolic with animal pleasure in the lukewarm, cloudy water. The unusually prolonged trip had forced us, imperceptibly, to set our own standards of living, and the whims of the climate, which made the untimely seasons follow one another with the speed of days and hours, added to the singular composition of our caravan; we had had to create a peculiar universe, as time passed, stranger and stranger than our way of life before departure. Although authority was relaxed, it was plain to see it was no longer necessary: In the fever of those unreal days, ordinary interests seemed to have disappeared. Only a few grudges remained: Siriri bitterly disapproved of our growing distance from the rules that had been instilled in him and which were his only reference for any possible world, and Suárez El Ñato, who did not stray from his master's wagon, like a faithful but slightly addled dog, signaled with his resentful gaze that, in his opinion, it was I, and not insanity, who was responsible for Troncoso's terrible collapse. But even his hatred, in that flat and yellow infinity, had lost its reins.

As Osuna announced the Santa Rosa storm for the thirtieth, we all kept watch for the saving clouds, eager but skeptical, to see if they were approaching our assembly from the southeast, laden less with water than with hope. But not a single cloud appeared in the first days of waiting. As we watched, the empty sky changed color with the passing light and lost its aura of familiarity, a consequence of our certainty that it had always been there; it became strange, and with it the yellow earth and all that spanned the visible horizon, including ourselves. The burnt and sweaty faces, in which the eyes were almost shrunken, mouth always open and brows always furrowed, expressed a constant questioning. At times we spoke little, exchanging shy monosyllables, and at others, usually in an aside among two or three, we exchanged long, fragmentary monologues, hurried and confused, as if in the plain's monotony we had lost the instinct or notion that separates the inner from the outer, as if the language provided in this world had also been uprooted from us and would have spoken for itself, doing without the thought and will with which we had learned to employ it on first entering this world.

At last, one afternoon, the clouds began to come. As it was still early, the first ones were large and very white, festooned with rippling edges, and when they passed too low, their own shadow would obscure their underside, as seen from the ground. We hoped before long to see them go black and part from the horizon in an endless slate-gray mass, to blot out all the sky and spill forth with rain. But for two days they paraded past in the sky, frayed and mute, coming from the southeast as I think I have said, and disappeared behind us to some point at our backs on an already-traveled horizon. They changed shape and color with the hours of the day and, above all, they floated at different speeds, as if the wind, whose absence we suffered on the ground, abounded there above. Sometimes they were yellow, orange, red, lilac, violet, but also green, gold, and even blue. Although they were all similar, there did not exist, nor had there ever existed since the origins of the world, nor would there exist either until the inconceivable end of time, two that were identical. With their varied forms and the recognizable shapes they portrayed, which dissolved little by little until they no longer looked like anything, or even assumed a shape contradictory to the one they had taken a moment before, they made me feel like a spirit of history, one that would persist through time to change along with the clouds, with the same strange similarity of such things that vanish, in the very instant they arise, to that place we call the past, where no one ever goes.

It will sound like fiction to my readers, but we awaited the water eagerly for days, and in place of water came fire. It was the twenty-ninth of August, 1804. If this precision awakens the suspicions of my potential reader, suggesting that I employ it to increase the illusion of truthfulness, I would like it to remain quite clear that this date is unforgettable for me, as it marks the most extraordinary day of my life.

For many hours, a strong smell of burning, which had grown stronger and more unmistakable, prompted comments in the caravan, but as no breeze was blowing and there were no visible signs of fire along the horizon, it proved difficult to identify the source of the smell. Osuna's concern, and his secret meetings with Sergeant Lucero and with Sirirí, were the only tangible proof to me that the invisible yet pervasive fire was very real, so when Sirirí left to explore southward and Osuna suggested we alter the course to the east a bit, I realized that the situation appeared far more serious to our experts than I had imagined. Osuna explained to me that if there was a fire, it might be coming from the south, which was why Sirirí had ridden that way—to determine at what distance it was coming up against us—and that the caravan was going east because the fire had less chance of spreading on the wetlands near the river. According to Osuna, if there was a fire, which was all but certain, the origin was likely some thunderbolt in one of those dry storms that sometimes advance a few days before the torrential rains that sweep down on the region. With regard to the fire, and always according to Osuna, it could be a small matter or, to the contrary, form a front for many leagues; the heat and dry grass would help it spread slowly in the absence of wind, but if by chance the southeaster that came to accompany the Santa Rosa storms began to blow, the speed of propagation would multiply in no time. Thus, Osuna and Lucero had taken the precaution of altering our route toward the river.

Osuna, glancing frequently and nervously to the south, meant for us to hurry, but, if I haven't said it before now, I believe that now is the time to point out that, though drawn by four horses and faster than ox-drawn freight wagons, even without considering the patients we were transporting, our carts moved quite slowly. Our trip had dragged on, not just because of the natural obstacles and incidents that delayed it, but also because of the slowness of the vehicles that made up the caravan, whose rhythm the horsemen escorting us had to adapt to. On the afternoon of the twenty-eighth, a few black clouds, thick and motionless, began to appear at our right, to the south, as we marched east. For a time, I thought it was the long-awaited storm brewing, but when Osuna and Lucero started badgering the cart-men to increase their pace, anxiously searching the black skeins that walled the horizon, I realized they were not clouds. As it darkened, the last ruddy gleam that always lingered on the plain after the sun disappeared kept burning through the night, taking up the entire southern horizon. In the very black, even darkness, the yellow points of distant stars seemed kindlier and more familiar than the fluctuating, reddened stripe that sketched the southeastern arc of the horizon with its broad strokes. For the first time since our departure, we did not halt that night save to change the spent horses. When dawn broke, sunlight blotted out the fire, but the masses of black smoke seemed taller and appeared to rise up like stones beyond the horizon, ominously close. The sergeant scrutinized them for a moment and said that if we continued east the fire would leave us no time to reach the river, and that we had to change direction again, retreating to the north. So we began to retrace our steps with the fire at our heels, and as I checked my horse from straying too far from my patients' wagons, the memory came to me of that enigmatic saying of the oriental sages: *He who draws near, is far.* It could have meant, in effect, that in some way we too were approaching our goal, backtracking a good part of the journey.

For all our speed, the wall of smoke always seemed the same distance away, and even, at times, appeared to come closer, as though it traveled more lightly than we did. In broad daylight, we could see we were not the only ones who fled: Wild animals, whose presence we constantly sensed but who rarely showed themselves, forgot age-old cautions and fled northward—and often, faster than the fire and us. There was a cloud of birds in the air above our heads, ringing continually with cries, caws, screeches, et cetera, but when I observed them for a moment I could tell that though many flew in the same direction as us, some seemed to be going to meet the fire. I thought they erred, disoriented by the blaze, but when the fire reached us a few hours later, I realized, and Osuna later confirmed, that certain birds would fly above the blaze to feed on the insects it dispersed in all directions, especially those crisped in the heat, doing so with such insistence, recklessness, and gluttony, that many of them fell, trapped in the flames.

At dusk we arrived at a large lake, which was situated a bit farther northeast of the northwest-to-southeast trajectory we had been following and thus had not had the opportunity to see in the preceding days. We worked our way around it, bringing it between the fire and ourselves and, exhausted, stopped to rest. The lake was vaguely oval-shaped, some three hundred meters long, and it extended parallel to the line of dark smoke that blocked out most of the horizon. Toward the center, the distance between the two banks must have come to approximately half its length. Neither men nor horses were inclined to press on, and many wild animals seemed to have made the same decision. Lapwings, rhea birds, hares, herons, guanacos, partridges, and even a couple of pumas patrolled the area surrounding the water. Although our presence disturbed them, they did not dare leave the lake; they kept their distance, and with what we might deem excellent logic (for I see no other way), they reasoned that we were less dangerous an enemy than the fire. The pumas upset the women, so two soldiers ran at them laughing, and though the pumas postured ferociously at first, when the soldiers came too close, waving their bolas, they ran off and stopped after a distance, spitting and shaking.

Rarely have I beheld a more beautiful evening, and on the plain such evenings abounded, with endless sunsets during which, without a single obstacle to interfere with the sight, even the faintest embers of light linger in the all-effacing darkness. When the sun's enormous disc met the eastern horizon, the yellow grass began to shimmer, seeming all the brighter in contrast to the wall of smoke to the south, while the red plate of the lake, reflecting the shifting light and undisturbed by the slightest vibration, went blue and finally black, as if it were cooling along with the light and the air, the sky, and such; only the crimson line on the southeast horizon introduced a certain variety in the night's uniform blackness.

If someone believes the travail we were undergoing could have left me time to admire the sunset, he would be wrong, for it was amid the general hustle and bustle, in which everyone, apart from the patients, had something to do, that such indifferent and superhuman twilit beauty took shape, reached perfection, and foundered in the night. Most judiciously, Osuna and the sergeant decided that since the men and animals were camped on the shore, the carts ought to be set up as far into the lake as possible, and this took a long while because we had to seek out the parts of the lake-bed where the weight would not bog down the wagons when the danger had passed and we wanted to remove them from the water. Indeed, a site far enough from the bank but not so deep that

153

the water would penetrate the wagons was a contradictory goal, difficult to meet. It was pitch-dark when we finished. The smell of burning filled the air, and, at a distance difficult to gauge, beyond the sunken carts out near the center of the lake, the red band of the blaze shone, flickering and faint.

We remained camped on the shore trying to make out, in the pitch dark, possible signs that would alert us to the fire's advance. As our eyes grew accustomed to the dark, we began to distinguish the weightier silhouettes of the things that populated the general blackness. The nurses and I had gathered our patients to better watch over them. After a period of darkness, several candles and lanterns were lit, but the sergeant advised they be extinguished to better scrutinize the horizon from a deeper darkness. He allowed me to leave a pair of candles lit so that we might better keep watch over our mad. In truth, the only ones from which I expected some unrest were the elder Verde and the little nun; Prudencio Parra remained as indifferent as ever to the vagaries of this world, and the only sign of aggravation he showed under the circumstances was the tightening of his fist, and while Troncoso made a few slight starts of agitation, it was clear that the gravest lay behind us and a new paroxysm was unlikely for the moment. Moreover, El Ñato would not be detached from him, so I was certain I could count on him if something urgent arose. The devoted servant protecting the disgraced master who in ordinary times would torture and humiliate him . . . It is an eternal paradox that provokes, and will provoke, the philosopher's eternal puzzlement. And with regard to Verdecito, there was no danger of losing sight of him amidst the general disorder, for not only did he stay by my side, he even clung to my shirtsleeve and would not let me go. He manifested his growing excitement in the multiplicity of sounds that left his lips, and, with an increasingly faint and shaky voice, he questioned me continually, such that even I, busy with the situation and intent on the outer world, could not understand him and answered without stopping to listen, especially in the direst of moments, with any old thing, which, as was his custom, he would make me repeat several times. Despite the increasing gravity of the situation, the nurses laughed at our deaf-men's dialogue. The brothers Verde, I must note, were the two most difficult problems to manage in those trying hours, for as the danger approached, so, too did the elder's excitement grow, and in tense moments, it was his perennial *morning, noon, and night,* spoken with the thousand different modulations of a normal conversation and directed to no one in particular, which was all that could be heard. The greater the peril, the stronger his voice rang out, and the more rapid the rhythm and variety of his utterances. Sister Teresita, who sometimes enjoyed pestering the two brothers, left them in peace that night, though her reasons were hardly commendable, for she passed a good part of the wait whispering and joking in the dark with the soldiers in her personal guard and, mostly because I thought the soldiers would see to her and protect her, I prudently refrained from discovering where those schemes might lead, even up to the point when, surrounded by the fire, we took shelter in the lake in water up to our necks because, in the part of the lake where she was squeezed in among the soldiers, splashes, cries, and all-too eloquent moans could be heard—and it is already known that, for mysterious reasons, danger may stimulate hedonism.

We were shaken by an unexpected fright when, almost immediately, an equally unexpected satisfaction made up for our shock. As we watched events unfold in near-perfect silence, alert and anxious, clustered on the lakeshore, we noticed a murmur that, at least for me, proved difficult to identify at first. It gradually coalesced into the pounding of cattle hooves as they sounded against the earth, just as a tumult of terrified lowing, each one closer than the last, filled the night air. Our main fear was that the cattle, which were of course fleeing the blaze, and which had to be in a rather large herd given the din they made, would stampede out of the blind terror that made them take flight into the dark, trampling over us. We heard the beasts approaching in the blackness when the first hooves touched water at some point on the lake's far edge, and the watery sounds of their legs, more than the terrified moos resounding in the night (I felt Verdecito's hand grasp yet more tightly at my shirtsleeve) made us think we would not escape catastrophe, when we realized the beasts were gradually going off to the western edge of the lake where there was more beach, some by water and others near the shore, until we heard them come across the lake and make off behind us, to the north, striking the earth with their hooves as they did. The explanation for that abrupt change of route came immediately, with the trot of a horse that drew near without difficulty, and which, with his gift for sounding the invisible, Osuna recognized by the hoof-beats as Sirirí's. Reining in sharply at a distance, the Indian identified himself in the darkness and joined us. By lantern-light and in the middle of a circle of anxious, weary faces, he told us with characteristic seriousness how he had gone half a league south of our camp when he heard the cattle rushing to the lake, and so racing flat-out on the diagonal, he intercepted the mob and diverted it to the western point of the lake. There were only a few cows, Sirirí said, and so perhaps they would not have caused much of a disaster apart from the carts, but they were so frightened that they made enough noise for many more than they were in reality. What follows should illustrate these men's skill for life on the plain, like sailors on the sea: Sirirí had agreed with Osuna and the sergeant to meet on the bank of the Paraná river, well to the east, but, after estimating the time it would take the fire to reach them and calculating the distance to the river, he had arrived at the same conclusion as the other two experts, deciding that the only place in the surroundings where we might defend ourselves from the blaze was that lake where we found ourselves. An important detail ought to be noted: Alone, Sirirí had been able to escape the fire with ease, as a rider can move about ten times faster than a convoy of carts. In little time, he had been able to gain such a lead on the fire that the blaze preparing to devour us had not posed the slightest danger to him. And nevertheless, knowing he would face the same danger as all of us, he returned to camp. Apart from the purely professional respect that Osuna and the sergeant perhaps deserved, none of the other members of the caravan roused the least sympathy. Over the month of our journey, Sirirí had heard us joke about him, had seen us trample the few things sacred to him in this world, the few truths in which, according to him, it was worth it to believe, and more than once, I had detected scorn, fury, and scandal written on his face when he judged some of our actions. And despite that, he endangered his life and came back to us. Likely, there was no doubt for him that the members of the caravan would burn for all eternity in the fires of hell; but in the face of the actual fire that approached, he had gone to our side.

At daybreak, the fire reached us. Protected by water, its age-old nemesis, we saw it stop and dance at the lakeshore. The front of the blaze stretched endlessly from east to west. The crackling flames were deafening, and greedy birds hurled themselves into clouds of smoke to eat the charred insects, excited by heat, danger, fire, and perhaps the abundance of food, letting out dreadful cries, unnatural in a bird, blackened by the night but suddenly illuminated by the flames' glow, seemingly and suddenly risen from another world, another time, another nature with different laws than our own. The blaze lit up the entire countryside, which took on the excessive brightness of a rather flashy party, and the flames doubled when reflected in the lake, whose waters had turned an undulating orange color, so we who were within

157

it, up to our necks in that reddened and flaming element, had the impression of being trapped in the very heart of the inferno, especially because, perhaps owing to the overheated earth and endless expanse of flames, our skin could detect the rise in water temperature to the point that we began to wonder—to ourselves, of course, for apart from the Verde brothers, who were impossible to silence, nobody spoke—whether it might begin to boil at any moment. The smoke, which at a distance appeared firm and sturdy as a wall, was a wildly writhing, turbulent fluid up close, and between its thick and agitated masses, changing color at every turn, furious columns of sparks and igneous material would rise up all at once to explode mid-air and split off in all directions like projectiles, flying and crackling over our heads or speeding past us, or into the water where they were extinguished and suddenly turned to tiny black bits that floated on the surface, or else, flying over the whole width of the lake, fell on the other side beyond the bank, where a number of little scattered fires had started to burn. Verdecito clasped at my neck and whispered incomprehensible phrases in my ear, one after another, but his older brother had stopped, fallen silent, and remained rigid and pale with terror, with the water up to his neck but his back to the flames, so as not to look at them.

It was difficult to estimate the width of that wall of fire; what is known is that the blaze hugged the shore of the lake and extended northward, so at a given point the lake's oval surface, with us inside it, the horses that a group of soldiers were trying at great pains to hold back (and only succeeding because they had hobbled and bound them), the dogs that had barked themselves weary, the wild animals that would not leave the water for anything in the world, and the birds flitting in the ruddy air, that watery mirror we had seen so placid and smooth at dusk, seemed an oval nightmare painted by a demented artist and framed in fire.

After a while, we realized daybreak had come but that the smoke was hiding the sunlight. And not only the smoke—as punctually as Osuna had announced, the Santa Rosa storms arrived from the southeast: It was the morning of the thirtieth. The fire passed by, continuing northward, and when the smoke began to clear, we saw the sky spotted with a few thick, blue-gray clouds. All around us, the blackened countryside was scattered with small, ruddy embers, like a night sky riddled with stars. From the ground, black as carbon, numerous little wisps of light and exhausted smoke sprouted, becoming invisible a meter up. We had not lost a single man, a single animal, a single cart. But although the fire had granted us a new term, now on its mindless northward way, we could not leave the water because the earth was still burning like the floor of a brick oven. The Basque climbed up on his cart, disappeared inside on all fours, and came back out with three bottles of gin, which he tossed in the air; the nimble soldiers, lively despite fatigue and the scorching heat, caught them. The bottles passed from hand to hand, and in no time their spirits were revived. Saved from the fire for unknowable reasons, they already had little to lose. By consuming us, the flames would have consumed our delirium as well, which was the only thing truly our own that distinguished us from the flat and silent land. And since the indifferent flames, almost scornful, had passed over without even stopping to destroy us, our delirium, intact, could begin to forge the world in its image again.

Heavy rain fell all day, pierced by fearsome lightning that was a new source of terror for us, and not only put out the embers and cooled the earth, but even restored the winter we had lost in the middle of our journey, having been upset by that improper summer's disruption of the natural order of the seasons. Now, with winter back in its place, we could wait for spring. For two or three days we traveled slowly across a dead, black, ashen land, which an icy drizzle soaked and turned to a runny mixture of carbonized grass, mud, and ash. The sky was just as black as the earth and the water fell unceasingly, gray and glacial. We rode, weary, focused, numb, and clumsy, a little unreal, having almost forgotten, after so many ordeals, the reason for our journey. But on the fourth day, the burnt countryside was left behind, and in the direction we traveled, always southeast, a few glimpses of tender green could be discerned among the dead grass of winter's end. On the fifth, the sun returned in a blue sky with not a cloud to be seen, and in the bright, rain-washed breeze, we encountered a few cow-herds, and in the afternoon we just made out the first farmhouses. People greeted us as we passed and stayed to watch because of our strange appearance—since, dirty and blackened by sun and by fire, smoke, and ash, dead-tired and wretched, we seemed neither bitter nor resigned. In the courtyards, peach trees, with their usual impatience, were full of pink flowers. I wished a little more for myself than at the start of the journey, and the world, contrary to all reason, seemed kind that day. The next morning, some five hundred meters from the river, above the ravine, we caught sight of a long, white building and, at its base, three tall acacia trees. As in the fourth Bucolic, the Fates, at last, decreed it.

Hilary Vaughn Dobel has an MFA in poetry and translation from Columbia University. She is the author of two manuscripts and, in addition to Juan José Saer, has translated work by Carlos Pintado.

OPEN LETTER

OPEN LETTER